# The Art of Balance
# Natural Healing for a Modern Life
# The Healing Kitchen

By Deidre Harvey

First Edition
ISBN: **9781970577112**
Cover design and layout by Deidre
For more information, contact: deidreharvey@hotmail.com

## Disclaimer

The information presented in this book is intended for educational and informational purposes only. It is not intended to diagnose, treat, cure, or prevent any disease, nor should it be considered as a substitute for professional medical advice, diagnosis, or treatment.

I am not a licensed medical doctor or healthcare provider. The insights and suggestions offered in this book are based on personal experience, research, and traditional practices and should not be interpreted as medical guidance.

Before making any changes to your health routine, including diet, supplements, detox practices, or the use of any therapies or devices mentioned herein, please consult with a qualified healthcare professional. Your health decisions are your own responsibility, and any application of the information provided in this book is done solely at your own risk.

Neither the author nor the publisher assumes any liability for possible adverse effects or consequences resulting from the use of any information contained in this book.

# Index:

# Dedication

This book is dedicated to those who feel alone, overwhelmed, confused, or even terrified.

Anyone who's walked the path of healing knows it's never the same for any two people. Each journey is unique. Each challenge personal. But one truth remains: you are not powerless, and you are not alone.

I was, and still am, fortunate. I had the most incredible support; my husband Gordon, daughters Roxanne and Danielle, their wonderful husbands Steve and Hilal, and my dear friend Andrea, who stood by me through every twist, turn, treatment, and moment of doubt. I'm also deeply grateful to the many others who offered wisdom, comfort, and strength when I needed it most.

Still, this book isn't just a thank you. It's a dedication to you, the reader who might be searching for answers, strength, or hope. I want you to know that healing is possible. That there is always support, even if it doesn't look the way you expected. And that within you lies more power, wisdom, and resilience than you may yet believe.

Stay curious. Stay grounded. Stay open. You are never walking this path alone.

*"You don't have to do it all today. You just have to take one small, loving step toward balance, and trust your body to meet you the*

# Foreward

This foreword is my story, my why, and how it led to the practices in this book. Feel free to read it now, or come back to it when the time is right.

A doctor once sat across from me, delivering words no one is ever prepared to hear.

"You have cancer," he said looking at me sadly. "I've treated two women with the exact same diagnosis, same type, same stage. One of them broke down in tears, slipped into depression, and began giving away her belongings. She believed it was the end and even though she went through chemotherapy and radiation, she didn't make it to five years."

He paused.

"The other woman was different. She transformed her life. During her treatments, she smiled, joked, and became a source of light for others. She's still alive and thriving."

And then he looked me in the eyes and said, "The choice is yours."

That was ten years ago.

Why am I still alive? I don't have all the answers, but I believe there are three reasons that shaped not only my survival, but my transformation.

The first is **purpose**. I've always felt there was unfinished business, threads of life still to be tied. I don't fear death, but the thought of leaving before completing what I came here to do drives me to live with intention and spiritual responsibility.

The second is **lifestyle**. Long before my diagnosis, I leaned toward natural health. My children were lovingly taken to homeopaths instead of doctors and given carrots instead of candy after dentist appointments. I've always trusted herbs over pills and sought to treat the root rather than mask symptoms. I respect modern medicine, it saves lives, but for everyday wellness, I trust the body's innate wisdom and the tools nature provides.

The third is **curiosity and belief**. My diagnosis didn't break me, it awakened me. I dove deeper into energy healing, oils, meditation, sound, and more. I didn't just try them, I lived them. And I came to believe, more than ever, that we are far more capable than we've been led to believe. Our minds are powerful, our bodies brilliantly designed, and the earth is overflowing with tools to support us.

Now, when someone tells me they're struggling, physically, emotionally, or mentally, I listen with my whole heart. I share what I've learned not as a prescription, but as a guide. Because there is no one-size-fits-all approach to healing. Life shifts. We grow. The key isn't perfection, it's having a toolkit to support you through it all.

That's what this book is about. Not flawless balance or quick fixes, but real-life resilience, self-trust, and a deeper connection to your body. Healing isn't something that happens to us, it's something we co-create, choice by choice, moment by moment.

This book is meant to live with you, grow with you, and support you. Use it as a journal. Write in it. Fold the corners. Scribble in the margins. Keep track of your meals, your symptoms, your progress. Let it become a record of your healing journey - a blueprint for your health.

# Introduction

Welcome to *The Art of Balance: Natural Healing for a Modern Life*, a five-part journey into whole-person wellness. This series was born from experience, shaped by research, and written from the heart. It's for those of us who are seeking a way to feel better, live better, and heal in a world that often feels too fast, too toxic, and too disconnected from what truly matters.

Each book in this series explores a different dimension of health and healing:

- Part One: The Healing Kitchen - Where Wellness Begins
- Part Two: Clearing the Hidden Heaviness - Detoxing Your Home and Body
- Part Three: The Inner Garden - Healing Through the Mind
- Part Four: Frequency and Energy Healing - Bridging the Mystical and the Measurable
- Part Five: Living in Balance - Physical Wellness and Whole Living

You don't need to read them in order, and you certainly don't need to be perfect to begin. You just need to be open to listening to your body, trusting your inner knowing, and making small, intentional choices that support your healing.

And so, we begin, quite simply, with food.

This part of the journey focuses on the kitchen: not just what's on your plate, but how food interacts with your body, your mood, your energy, and your healing. Food can be medicine. It can also be stress, confusion, or overload. My goal here is to bring you back to clarity. To nourishment. To trust.

We'll explore how the food you eat affects inflammation, immunity, digestion, hormones, and even your thoughts. We'll talk about hydration, herbs, detoxing through diet, and the power of simple ingredients. We'll also make space for your intuition, because the best healing always includes listening to what your body is asking for. Whether you're just starting your wellness journey or are already deep in the process of reclaiming your health, let this be a gentle, grounding start. One ingredient, one meal, one loving choice at a time.

# Chapter One: Why Are You Here?

This book found you for a reason. Maybe you were seeking it, or perhaps it arrived quietly, like a key turning a lock you didn't know was waiting.

You're here searching for something: relief, insight, transformation, or simply a breath of hope. This isn't about telling you what to want, it's about uncovering what you already carry within.

Every cell in your body, and there are *trillions* of them, wants to *live*.

Yet somewhere along the way, you were taught to distrust this genius. To outsource your healing. To fear symptoms instead of listening to them.

✍ **Put your hand on your heart. Ask:**

*When did I last trust my body's voice?*

_______________________________________________

_______________________________________________

*What if "symptoms" are my cells' Morse code for help?*

_______________________________________________

_______________________________________________

*How would I treat myself if I believed healing was my birthright?*

_______________________________________________

_______________________________________________

Long before modern medicine, traditional healers observed consistent patterns in how the body responds to care and stress.

These observations formed the basis of holistic frameworks rooted in natural hygiene philosophy, approaches that are not universally accepted as medical doctrine.

**Dr. Herbert Shelton** called them *"The Hygienic System"* (1934), but their roots stretch back to Hippocrates.

## "The Seven Laws of the Body"

### ⚕ The Law of Self-Healing
The body always strives to maintain and restore health

### 🌿 The Law of Vital Economy
The body conserves and directs energy where it is most needed

### 🌀 The Law of Unity
The body operates as an integrated whole

### 🛏 The Law of Rest and Recuperation
Rest is essential for healing and regeneration

### ⚖ The Law of Cause and Effect
Every symptom has a cause.  Remove the cause that the symptom (effect) disappears

### 🦎 The Law of Adaptation
The body adapts to the conditions its exposed to, often at a cost.

### The Law of Purification
Toxins must be expelled, not repressed

**Healing begins with honesty. So let's start by asking:**

**What do I truly want for myself?**

Pause. Breathe. Let these questions open doors rather than demand answers. You don't have to solve anything yet. Just be curious.

*Read the statements and see what resonates with you:*

**Health & Vitality**

- ☐ Are you feeling exhausted, in pain, or disconnected from your body?
- ☐ Do you want to feel lighter, stronger, and more like yourself again?
- ☐ Are you searching for natural, sustainable ways to support your health?
- ☐ Are you overwhelmed by the many healing options and unsure where to begin?

*What does health truly mean to me?*

*How would it feel to trust my body again?*

## Body Image & Self-Acceptance.

*When have I felt most at home in my body?*

_______________________________________________

_______________________________________________

*What would shift if I felt that way again?*

_______________________________________________

_______________________________________________

*What messages have I absorbed about my body, and are they truly mine?*

_______________________________________________

_______________________________________________

## <u>Stress & Rest</u>

**Are you***:*

- [ ] Feeling overwhelmed, anxious, or emotionally drained?
- [ ] Is your nervous system constantly on edge, like it can't catch a break?
- [ ] Lying awake despite exhaustion?
- [ ] Waking up more tired than when you went to bed?
- [ ] Is something quietly worrying you, stealing rest from your nights and energy from your days?

***What does deep, nourishing rest look like for me?***

__________________________________________________________

__________________________________________________________

***Where do I need to give myself permission to pause?***

__________________________________________________________

__________________________________________________________

***What am I carrying, mentally or emotionally, that I can safely set down, even for a little while?***

__________________________________________________________

__________________________________________________________

***What's one way I can invite more rest into my daily rhythm?***

__________________________________________________________

__________________________________________________________

## Confidence & Inner Strength

*What made me feel confident before, and what small step could reconnect me to that now?*

_______________________________________________

_______________________________________________


## Purpose & Spiritual Connection

**Are you:**
- ☐ Sensing something's missing, even if life looks "fine"?
- ☐ Yearning for deeper meaning or alignment?
- ☐ Drawn to holistic healing, energy work, or self-discovery?

*What has my soul always nudged me to explore?*

_______________________________________________

_______________________________________________


*What am I most curious to learn about myself or healing?*

_______________________________________________

_______________________________________________


**Your Personal Compass.**
*If my body could speak, what would it ask me for, and how would it feel to give it that?*

_______________________________________________

_______________________________________________

<u>**Confidence & Purpose**</u>

*Where do I feel small or unseen?*

__________________________________________________________________

__________________________________________________________________

*When did I last feel fully aligned with myself*

__________________________________________________________________

__________________________________________________________________

<u>**My Toolkit (So Far)**</u>:

*What practices have helped me before? What am I open to trying?*

__________________________________________________________________

__________________________________________________________________

**My Top three Intentions for This Journey:**
*What three things I can start doing right now to achieve them?*

__________________________________________________________________

__________________________________________________________________

__________________________________________________________________

__________________________________________________________________

**A Final Note**. Return to these reflections anytime. Your answers may change, *because you will*. Healing isn't linear; it spirals and unfolds in seasons.

We'll explore nutrition, rest, detox, energy healing, and more in the chapters ahead, but for now, simply listen inward.

This is your beginning. Trust the process.

You are exactly where you need to be.

# Chapter Two: Let Food Be Your Foundation

When people ask me, "Where do I even begin?" I always say the same thing; start with food.

Not a diet. Not a cleanse. Just food. Real food. The kind that grows, breathes, and doesn't come with a label full of things you can't pronounce.

If you had to choose between a slice of cheesy, gooey pizza and a bowl of perfectly ripe fruit, what would you pick? And there's no shame in that. It's not a lack of willpower, it's clever chemistry.

Most of us are drawn to the pizza. And not because fruit isn't sweet, beautiful, or nourishing, but because our taste buds (and brains) have been hijacked. Years of processed, chemical-laced, hyper-palatable foods have rewired what we crave.

Think about it: "Fast food" should be an apple. Or a banana. Or a handful of berries.

Somehow, fast food became a symbol of convenience and comfort, but what it really is, is overprocessed, fake, chemical-ridden, sugar-laden, fried-up stuff that leaves us tired, bloated, and strangely wanting more.

Now, I'm not going to give you a whole long list of additives, preservatives, E-numbers, MSG, high-fructose corn syrup, artificial colours, seed oils, emulsifiers, stabilizers, and mystery "flavours." But I do suggest that you do.

Next time you're in the supermarket, take a look at what's actually in the tinned, bottled, and packaged food you're buying.

Then, do yourself a favour and walk straight to the vegetable aisle. Just stand there for a second. Notice the colours, the shapes, the freshness. That's what real food looks like. And it's a good place to start.

Food is one of the few things you can begin changing today.

Before the diagnosis. Before the crisis. Before the rock bottom moment. Every bite you take is a message to your body, one of stress or one of support. Of disconnection or nourishment.

And the beautiful thing is: your body responds almost immediately. It doesn't hold grudges.  It will forgive all the sugar, wheat, seed oils and other choices from the past, and simply work with what you give it moving forward. In fact, you can build an entirely new body over time.

Let's take a look at how long it takes to renew and regenerate:

- **Skin: 27 days**. Your skin cells are constantly shedding and being replaced.
- **Liver: 5 months to 1 year**. The liver is incredibly resilient and can regenerate itself even after significant damage.
- **Kidneys & Adrenals: 6 to 8 months**. These organs filter waste and regulate hormones, and with proper care, they can gradually rebuild function.
- **Pancreas: 6 to 12 weeks**. The pancreas, which plays a key role in blood sugar regulation, can improve its function with dietary and lifestyle changes.
- **Heart: 4.5 to 5 years**. While heart cells regenerate slowly, the heart can heal and strengthen over time with consistent healthy habits.
- **Stomach Lining: 5 days**. This area turns over quickly to handle acids and digestion.
- **Lungs: 2 to 3 weeks** for airway lining. Longer for full lung tissue healing, depending on lifestyle.
- **Red Blood Cells: 4 months.** Your entire blood supply is regularly renewed with old red blood cells continuously replaced.

- **White Blood Cells: 1 year.** These regenerate more slowly and are critical for your immune defense and fighting infection.
- **Bones: 10 years**. Your skeleton is constantly breaking down and rebuilding, albeit slowly. It typically takes 6 to 8 weeks for a broken bone to repair.
- **Brain: Ongoing**. Some neurons never regenerate, but the hippocampus (involved in memory) can produce new cells even into adulthood.

So yes, your body is always healing, always rebuilding. Give it the tools it needs, and it will do the rest. And it starts with feeding the  trillions of tiny cells. Every cell wants to survive and relies on you to put the correct nutrients in and on your body to function, repair, protect, and thrive. Think of nutrients as the raw materials of health, the bricks and mortar of your body's foundation.

**Testing for Imbalances: What's Really Going On?**

The first step to balancing your body is understanding where you are right now.  If you're already making good food choices but still feel off, functional testing can help you decode the mystery. Consider:

- **Oligoscan**. A non-invasive scan to assess heavy metal and mineral imbalances though the skin.
- **Hair Tissue Mineral Analysis (HTMA)**. Uses a small hair sample to provide a comprehensive mineral report.
- **Micronutrient Panels (blood test)**. Evaluates vitamins, minerals, amino acids, and antioxidants.

*✨ You don't need every test, but knowing your starting point and baseline is both powerful and practical. It helps you pinpoint what your body needs and gives you the information to make targeted nutrition decisions.*

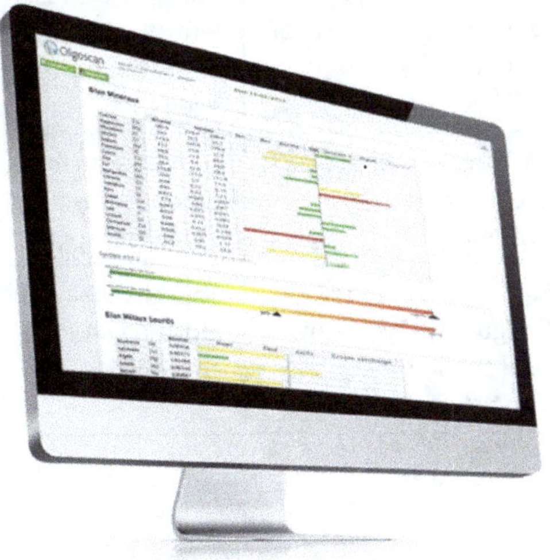

*Oligoscan Results*

## Essential Nutrients & Where to Find Them

These nutrients are the building blocks of health. Let's look at what they do, how deficiencies show up, and where to get them from whole foods.

| Nutrient/Purpose | Signs of Deficiency | Sources |
|---|---|---|
| **Magnesium:** Crucial for muscle function, nerve regulation, sleep, mood, and energy production. | Muscle cramps, anxiety, fatigue, sleep issues, migraines. | Leafy greens, pumpkin seeds, almonds, dark chocolate, avocados, bananas. |
| **Potassium:** Regulates fluid balance, heart rhythm, and nerve signalling. | Fatigue, high blood pressure, muscle weakness, irregular heartbeat. | Sweet potatoes, spinach, beans, coconut water, bananas, apricots. |
| **Zinc:** Vital for immunity, wound healing, and DNA synthesis. | Frequent colds, poor wound healing, loss of taste or smell. | Pumpkin seeds, lentils, chickpeas, cashews, oysters, eggs. |
| **Iron:** Enables oxygen transport throughout the body. | Fatigue, shortness of breath, pale skin, brain fog. | Lentils, spinach, quinoa, grass-fed red meat, pumpkin seeds. |
| **Iodine:** Essential for thyroid hormone production and metabolic health. | **Signs of deficiency:** Fatigue, weight gain, cold sensitivity, sluggish metabolism. | **Sources:** Seaweed, iodized salt, eggs, cranberries, fish. |

**Trace Minerals. The Micronutrient Heroes**

There are around 72 trace minerals in the body, all needed to keep us in balance and healthy.

Even in tiny amounts, minerals like selenium, manganese, molybdenum, boron, and chromium play vital roles in energy production, hormone balance, detoxification, and more.

*Many people are low in these trace nutrients without even realising it. Over farmed soils and processed foods often strip them out.*

**Making Healthy Food Choices**

Forget rules. Forget fads. Think of food as information. Whole, unprocessed, naturally grown foods tell your body, *"I've got your back."*

Simple Principles for Everyday Eating:

- **Colour = Nutrients**. The more colourful your meal, the more nutrients you're getting.
- **Whole is better**. Eat food that looks like it used to grow. Keep ingredient lists short and recognizable.
- **Fat is your friend**, Healthy fats (avocado, olive oil, coconut, nuts, seeds) help you absorb vitamins and stay full.
- **Read labels**. Sugar hides in many "healthy" snacks.
- **Hydrate!** Dehydration can feel like fatigue, hunger, brain fog, or even anxiety. Water is medicine.

This section is your go-to companion for understanding core food groups. Explore what they offer, how much to aim for, and how to bring them into your daily rhythm. Each page is a gentle prompt to observe, reflect, and experiment with what works for your body and lifestyle.

## ✏️Your Current Eating Habits

Before we dive deeper, take a moment to check in with where you are right now. Healing doesn't start with a perfect plan. it starts with awareness. Use the prompts below to reflect honestly and kindly.

There's no judgment here, just curiosity. This is your body's story. Let's listen.

***What does a typical day of eating look like for me right now?***

_______________________________________________

_______________________________________________

***How do I feel physically after eating: energised, tired, bloated, light?***

_______________________________________________

_______________________________________________

***Do I eat with intention or on autopilot?***

_______________________________________________

_______________________________________________

***Which foods do I crave most often, and when?***

_______________________________________________

_______________________________________________

***What role does food play in my emotional world?***

_______________________________________________

_______________________________________________

*Based on what I have just read and written, what changes do I want to make to my daily food choices?*

_________________________________________________

_________________________________________________

_________________________________________________

_________________________________________________

_________________________________________________

_________________________________________________

_________________________________________________

_________________________________________________

_________________________________________________

*If I nourished my body with healthy food for 30 days, what changes would I hope to see or feel?*

_________________________________________________

_________________________________________________

**Fruit & Vegetables**

*These colourful, living foods are nature's pharmacy. Full of life force, they feed every cell.*

➤ **What They Are:**
Leafy greens, root vegetables, berries, citrus fruit, cruciferous veg, stone fruit and more. Each colour signals different nutrients.  Eat the rainbow!

➤ **Benefits:**
Every single fruit and vegetable has a multitude of benefits:
- Rich in antioxidants, vitamins, and hydration
- Support gut health and gentle detox
- Lower risk of chronic illness
- Naturally energising and protective

➤ **Ideas for Use:**
- ☐ Morning smoothie or fruit bowl
- ☐ Raw snacks or crudités with dips
- ☐ Steamed or roasted with herbs
- ☐ Stirred into soups, stews, or grains
- ☐ Homemade juice or herbal blend (limit sweet fruit)

*What are your all-time favourite fruit?* Why do you love them - taste, texture, how they make you feel?

___________________________________________________

___________________________________________________

*What are your all-time favourite vegetables?* Why do you love them - taste, texture, how they make you feel?

___________________________________________________

___________________________________________________

**How do you currently include fruit and vegetables in your daily routine?** *Think about meals, snacks, drinks, or even desserts.*

___________________________________________________

___________________________________________________

**Are there any fruit or vegetables that your body seems to crave?** *What do you think it's trying to tell you?*

___________________________________________________

___________________________________________________

**What's one new fruit or vegetable you'd love to try but haven't yet?** *What's stopped you so far? How could you make it fun?*

___________________________________________________

___________________________________________________

**Which veggies do you wish you liked more?** *Could you prepare them in a new way; roasted, blended, grilled, or spiced?*

___________________________________________________

___________________________________________________

**Do you notice a difference in your energy or mood on days you eat more plants?** *Describe what changes you observe in your body.*

___________________________________________________

___________________________________________________

**Sprouts & Microgreens**

➤ **What They Are:**
Super tasty young seedlings of vegetables, beans, or grains. Includes broccoli sprouts, alfalfa, mung bean, radish, sunflower, and pea shoots.

➤ **Benefits:**
- Very high in antioxidants and enzymes
- Enhance detox and cellular regeneration
- Rich in chlorophyll, vitamins C and K
- Support digestion and immune health

➤ **Ideas for Use:**
- ☐ Add to salads or sandwich toppings
- ☐ Blend into smoothies for a green boost
- ☐ Use as a garnish on warm bowls or soups
- ☐ Toss with lemon, olive oil, and sea salt
- ☐ Grow your own on a windowsill for freshness and fun

Adding living foods like **sprouts** and **microgreens** to your diet is one of the simplest, most powerful ways to boost nutrition, energy, and healing. These tiny plants are rich in enzymes, antioxidants, vitamins, and minerals, far more concentrated than their mature versions.

Best of all, you can grow them at home on your kitchen windowsill with very little effort.

**Best Seeds to Use For Sprouting:**

- Mung beans
- Alfalfa
- Lentils
- Broccoli
- Radish
- Fenugreek
- Quinoa
- Chickpeas

**How to Grow Sprouts - You'll Need:**
- Organic sprouting seeds (e.g., mung beans, alfalfa, lentils, broccoli)
- Sprouting jar with mesh lid or a sprouting container (stacked trays)
- Filtered water

**Step-by-Step Instructions:**
1. **Soak Seeds:** Place 1 - 2 tablespoons of seeds in the sprouting container or jar. Add enough water to cover them and soak for 8 - 12 hours.
2. **Drain and Rinse:** After soaking, drain the water. Rinse with fresh water and drain again.
   Place the container upside down or angled to allow airflow and drainage.
3. **Rinse Twice Daily:** Rinse the sprouts morning and evening. Keep in a cool, dark area until tails emerge, then move to indirect light to green them.
4. **Harvest:** In 3 - 5 days, when tails are ¼ - ½ inch long, your sprouts are ready. Rinse one final time, drain well, and store in the fridge.

**Let's have a quick look at what is in these amazing plants:**

| Sprout | Key Properties | Health Benefits |
| --- | --- | --- |
| **Mung Bean** | Protein, vitamin C, potassium, fibre, B vitamins | Boosts immunity, improves skin, aids digestion, regulates blood sugar |
| **Alfalfa** | Vitamin K, C, phytoestrogens, saponins | Balances hormones, reduces inflammation, supports heart health, detoxifies |
| **Lentil** | Protein, iron, folate, prebiotic fibre | Enhances energy, supports gut health, good during pregnancy |
| **Broccoli** | Protein, vitamins A, C, and K | Liver detox, cancer prevention, brain and heart health, immune support |
| **Radish** | Spicy flavour, vitamin C, folate | Supports liver/gallbladder, aids digestion, antimicrobial, respiratory support |
| **Fenugreek** | Bitter, high in fibre, iron, and phytoestrogens | Balances hormones, aids lactation, regulates blood sugar, improves digestion |
| **Quinoa** | Protein, magnesium, phosphorus, fibre | Boosts metabolism, heart/bone health, gluten-free, easy to digest |

*Have you tried adding sprouts or microgreens to your meals? What drew you to them?*

_______________________________________________

_______________________________________________

*Based on what you have read, are there any you are keen to try?*

_______________________________________________

_______________________________________________

*How will you use them? (Eat as is. Add to salad, smoothie, soup, etc)*

_______________________________________________

_______________________________________________

*Will you grow them? (Can you picture them growing on our kitchen window sill?)*

_______________________________________________

_______________________________________________

**Nuts & Seeds**

*Just a handful holds minerals, healthy fats, and steady energy.*

➤ **What They Are:**
Plant-based sources of essential fats, fibre, and protein. Includes **almonds, walnuts, flax, chia, pumpkin seeds, sunflower seeds**, etc.

➤ **Key Properties and Benefits:**

| <u>Nut/Seed</u> | <u>Key Properties</u> | <u>Health Benefits</u> |
|---|---|---|
| **Almonds** | Rich in vitamin E, magnesium, healthy fats, protein, fibre | Brain health, skin health, blood sugar regulation, heart health |
| **Walnuts** | High in omega-3 fatty acids, antioxidants, melatonin | Brain function, inflammation, sleep, heart |
| **Flaxseeds** | Phytoestrogen, omega-3s, soluble fibre | Hormones, digestion, cholesterol, anti-cancer properties |
| **Chia Seeds** | High in omega-3s, calcium, magnesium, protein, fibre | Hydration, energy, bone health, weight management |
| **Pumpkin Seeds** | Rich in zinc, magnesium, iron, antioxidants, amino acid | Immune, prostate, sleep, combats fatigue |
| **Sunflower Seeds** | High in vitamin E, selenium, B vitamins, healthy fats | Skin, inflammation, thyroid and cardiovascular health |

➤ **Ideas for Use:**

☐ Sprinkle on oats, salads, or yogurt
☐ Blend into smoothies or nut/seed milks
☐ Make energy bites or homemade trail mix
☐ Stir into baking or pancake mix
☐ Add to warm grain bowls

*What nuts or seeds do you currently use?*

_______________________________________________

_______________________________________________

*What nuts or seeds have you not tried?*

_______________________________________________

_______________________________________________

*Have you ever looked into the nutritional and healing properties of nuts and seeds?*

_______________________________________________

_______________________________________________

## Proteins: Plant & Animal

*Proteins are the builders of muscle, enzymes, hormones, and resilience.*

### ➤ What They Are:
Vital macronutrients found in eggs, meat, fish, dairy, tofu, legumes, nuts, quinoa, edamame, chickpeas, chia seeds and some fermented foods.

| Food | Key Properties | Health Benefits |
|---|---|---|
| Eggs | High quality protein, choline, vitamin B12, selenium | Brain and eye health, builds muscle, aids metabolism |
| Meat | Complete protein, iron, B vitamins, zinc | Builds muscle, red blood cell formation, boosts energy |
| Fish | Omega-3 fatty acids, protein, vitamin D, iodine | Heart and brain health, anti-inflammatory, thyroid and vision |
| Dairy | Calcium, protein, vitamin D, B12, potassium | Strong bones and teeth, muscle growth, gut health |
| Tofu | Plant-based protein, calcium, iron, isoflavones: phytoestrogens | Hormonal balance, heart health, bone density, low in calories |
| Legumes | Fibre, protein, folate, iron, magnesium | Digestion, blood sugar, heart-healthy, weight management |
| Edamame | Young soybeans, rich in protein, fibre, folate, vitamin K | Muscle maintenance, hormone regulation, bone health, cholesterol |
| Chickpeas | Protein, fibre, folate, iron, complex carbs | Blood sugar, digestion, increases satiety |

➤ **Ideas for Use:**

☐ Grilled or baked with herbs and lemon
☐ Stirred into broths, stews, or veggie bowls
☐ Protein-rich smoothies (plant or whey based)
☐ Pair plant proteins for full amino acid range (e.g., beans + rice

*What is your 'go to' form of protein?*

__________________________________________________

__________________________________________________

*How often do you eat protein a day?  For which meals?*

__________________________________________________

__________________________________________________

*Would you consider using plant based proteins?  Which?*

__________________________________________________

__________________________________________________

**Beans, Lentils & Legumes**

*These humble staples are slow burning, nourishing, and sustainable.*

➤ **What They Are:**
Edible seeds like black beans, lentils, chickpeas, kidney beans, peas, and soy. High in plant protein, minerals, and complex carbs.

| Food | Key Properties | Health Benefits |
|---|---|---|
| **Black Bean** | Fibre, protein, folate and antioxidants, | Digestion, blood sugar regulation and heart health |
| **Kidney Beans** | Fibre, protein and slow digesting carbs | Weight management, blood sugar and colon health |
| **Peas** | Fibre, vitamins A,C,K and protein | Immunity, vision and digestion |
| **Soy** | Complex protein, isoflavones and calcium | Bone health, hormonal balance and heart health |

➤ **Ideas for Use:**
☐ Make lentil or black bean soups
☐ Add to salads, wraps, or nourish bowls
☐ Mash into spreads (like hummus)
☐ Try bean-based pastas or stews
☐ Use in veggie burgers or patties

**How does your body respond to legumes?** Any favourites? Do they sit well or cause any bloating or discomfort?

_______________________________________________

_______________________________________________

**Do you enjoy the taste?** Describe the flavour. Describe the flavour, texture, and your overall impression.

_______________________________________________

_______________________________________________

**Which legumes would you try again, and with what foods?** Note any pairings or recipes you'd like to explore again.

_______________________________________________

_______________________________________________

**Which legumes are you happy to avoid, and why?** Reflect on any that didn't work well for your body or palate. Reflect on any that didn't work well for your body or palate.

_______________________________________________

_______________________________________________

**Healthy Fats & Oils**

*Good fats are your friends! They don't make you fat, help your brain fire, your cells communicate, and your skin glow.*

➤ **What They Are:**
Nourishing fats found in olive oil, avocado, coconut oil, flaxseed oil, ghee, nut butters, and oily fish (like salmon and sardines).

| Food | Key Properties | Main Benefits |
|---|---|---|
| **Olive Oil** | Monounsaturated fats, antioxidants, and anti-inflammatory compounds | Heart health, reduces inflammation, protects cells from oxidation |
| **Avocado** | Healthy fats, fibre, potassium, and vitamins E, C, B6 | Skin health, heart health, hormone balance |
| **Coconut Oil** | Medium-chain triglycerides (MCTs) and lauric acid | Boosts energy, supports metabolism, antimicrobial properties |
| **Flaxseed Oil** | Alpha-linolenic acid (ALA), a plant-based omega-3 fatty acid | Brain and heart health, reduces inflammation |
| **Ghee** | Clarified butter rich in fat-soluble vitamins (A, D, E, K) and butyrate | Supports gut lining, digestion, joint health |
| **Nut Butters** | Healthy fats, protein, fibre, and minerals (magnesium, zinc) | Supports energy, satiety, muscle and nerve function |
| **Oily Fish** | Omega-3 fatty acids (EPA & DHA), vitamin D, and high quality protein | Brain function, reduces inflammation, protects heart health |

➤ **Ideas for Use:**

☐ Drizzle extra virgin olive oil over salads or steamed veggies
☐ Mash avocado on toast with lemon and herbs
☐ Stir ghee or coconut oil into warm grains or soups
☐ Add flaxseed oil to smoothies (don't heat)
☐ Snack on oily fish or use nut butter in snacks

***How do you feel when you include good fats?*** *Any changes in mood, skin, or focus?*

______________________________________________

______________________________________________

**Do you feel more energised or stable throughout the day?** Observe if good fats help you feel more nourished or reduce energy crashes.

______________________________________________

______________________________________________

**Have you noticed any improvements in focus or brain clarity?** Some fats (like omega-3s) support brain function. Did you feel a difference?

______________________________________________

______________________________________________

**How is your skin responding?** Are you seeing improvements in hydration, texture, or breakouts?

______________________________________________

______________________________________________

**Which healthy fats do you enjoy most - and why?** Are there specific oils, spreads, or foods that your body loves?

______________________________________________

______________________________________________

**Are there any fats that you didn't respond well to?** Note any heaviness, indigestion, or allergic-type reactions.

---

🦷 **Bonus Tip: Try Oil Pulling for Oral Detox**

**Oil pulling** is an ancient Ayurvedic practice that helps cleanse the mouth, improve gum health, and even support whole-body wellness.

🥥 **How to Do It:**

1  **Choose your oil:** Use 1 tablespoon of **coconut oil**, **sesame oil**, or **castor oil** (coconut is most popular).
2  **Swish:** Gently swish the oil in your mouth for **10 - 20 minutes**. Do **not swallow**.
3  **Spit:** When done, **spit the oil into a tissue or bin**, **not the sink**, as it can clog plumbing.
4  **Rinse & brush:** Rinse your mouth with warm water and brush your teeth as usual.

🌿 **Benefits of Oil Pulling:**

- Reduces harmful oral bacteria and plaque
- Supports gum health and fresher breath
- May reduce inflammation throughout the body
- Can whiten teeth naturally over time

♻️ **Disposal Tip:** Always **spit the used oil into a paper towel or jar** and throw it in the trash. Avoid pouring it down the sink as it can solidify and cause blockages.

## Whole Grains

*Whole grains carry the strength and stability of the seed. They are grounding, energising, and sustaining.*

➤ **What They Are:** Unrefined grains that retain the bran, germ,  and endosperm. Includes oats, brown rice, quinoa, millet, barley, bulgur, and whole wheat.

| Grain | Key Properties | Main Benefits |
|---|---|---|
| **Oats** | High in soluble fibre (beta-glucan), protein, and B vitamins | Supports heart health, lowers cholesterol, and stabilizes blood sugar |
| **Brown Rice** | Whole grain rich in fibre, selenium, magnesium, and antioxidants | Aids digestion, supports energy metabolism, and reduces inflammation |
| **Millet** | Gluten-free, rich in magnesium, phosphorus, and antioxidants | Supports bone health, cardiovascular function, and is easy to digest |
| **Barley** | High in both soluble and insoluble fibre, selenium, and B vitamins | Supports digestion, heart health, and blood sugar balance |
| **Bulgur** | Quick-cooking whole grain, rich in fibre and plant-based iron | Supports digestive health and sustained energy release |
| **Whole Wheat** | Contains fibre, iron, B vitamins, and complex carbohydrates | Promotes satiety, supports digestion, and provides long-lasting energy |

➤ **Ideas for Use:**
☐ Warm porridge with fruit and seeds
☐ Whole grain salads with herbs and lemon
☐ Add to soups or nourish bowls
☐ Try sprouted or fermented grain breads
☐ Use as a base for stir-fries or roasted veggies

***Caution: Be Mindful of Modern Grains***

*Many grains today are genetically modified (GM)* **or** *processed with additives, preservatives, or sprayed with glyphosate (a common pesticide). These can sometimes trigger inflammation, digestive issues, or immune reactions, especially to sensitive individuals.*

**Tip: Whenever possible, choose:**

- **Organic** and **non-GMO** varieties
- **Whole, sprouted,** or **stone-ground** grains
- Grains in their **least processed form**

Listening to your body and reading ingredient labels can help you enjoy grains that nourish rather than deplete.

Growing up as one of eight children, I could tell the day of the week just by the breakfast porridge on the table, a talent I never asked for, and one that hasn't always come with fond memories. Some days were definitely less popular than others!

**Does it bring back memories from childhood?** Are there grains that remind you of family meals, cultural traditions, or comfort foods?

_______________________________________________

_______________________________________________

**Explore: Which grains make you feel most grounded and energised?** Notice which ones give you lasting energy without making you feel heavy or sluggish.

_______________________________________________

_______________________________________________

**How does your body respond to different grains?** Pay attention to digestion, bloating, mental clarity, or any signs of inflammation.

_______________________________________________

_______________________________________________

**How do you like your grains prepared?** Do you enjoy them warm and soft, chewy, in soups, or in baked dishes?

_______________________________________________

_______________________________________________

**Have you tried sprouted or fermented grains?** Did you notice a difference in how your body tolerated them?

_______________________________________________

_______________________________________________

 **Eat the Rainbow: Colour as a Nutritional Guide**

To simplify eating, use colour to balance eating habits.

| Colour | Benefits | Examples |
|---|---|---|
| Red | Heart health, skin, cancer protection | Tomatoes, strawberries, beets |
| Orange/Yellow | Eye health, immunity, anti-inflammatory | Carrots, turmeric, mango |
| Green | Detox, gut healing, cancer prevention | Kale, avocado, matcha |
| Blue/Purple | Brain boost, anti-aging, longevity | Blueberries, purple cabbage |
| White/Brown | Immune support, bone health | Garlic, mushrooms, onions |
| Black | Gut health, detox, minerals | Black sesame, black rice |

**Colour-Based Meal Tips:**

1. **Eat 3 Colours Per Meal.** Ensures nutrient diversity.
2. **Rainbow Bowls.** Create meals by layering colourful ingredients like Buddha bowls.

**Targeted Nutrition: What Do You Want to Achieve?**

**Use tools like Google or ChatGPT to explore the concept of food as medicine for specific health goals.** For example, you might search: *"Natural foods that help reduce tumour growth."*

*What I want to heal:*
_______________________________________

*Foods:* _______________________________________
_______________________________________
_______________________________________

*How to Use them:* _______________________________________
_______________________________________
_______________________________________
_______________________________________

*What I want to heal:*
_______________________________________

*Foods:* _______________________________________
_______________________________________
_______________________________________

*How to Use them:* _______________________________________
_______________________________________
_______________________________________
_______________________________________

**Here's how I incorporate healing foods: Everyday Applications:**

1. **Turmeric** (Always pair with black pepper) - Fresh, in shots, golden tea at night, or added to meals.
2. **Leafy Greens** - In smoothies, juices, salads, or steamed.
3. **Green Tea with Lemon** - Boosts flavour and effectiveness.
4. **Medicinal Mushrooms (Reishi, Chaga, Turkey Tail)** - In food, powdered, or as tinctures.
5. **Pomegranate** - Great for brain and body. Snack, salad topping, or smoothie addition if you don't mind a few hard bits.
6. **Flaxseed** - Particularly powerful in hormone-related conditions. Add to smoothies or mix with cottage cheese.
7. **Berries** - Versatile, powerful, and easy to snack on.
8. **Garlic** - Cooked, raw, or fermented for extra benefits.

*The goal isn't to change your life overnight, just to make sustainable changes wherever you can.*

**A Gentle Invitation**

You don't need to change everything at once. Start small:
- Swap one snack.
- Add one extra veggie.
- Drink one more glass of water.
- Read one label.
- Get curious.

*Your body is always listening. It will notice. And it will thank you.*

**Incorporating Healthy Foods into Your Daily Meals**

As someone who would probably rather starve than cook, find buddha bowl-style meals a brilliantly easy way to get maximum nutrition, without even going near a stove.

***No-Cook Buddha Bowl*** (Vibrant, Fresh & Nourishing)
**Base (Choose One)**
- 1 cup pre-cooked quinoa, brown rice, or couscous
- Veggies (Raw & Crunchy)

**Pick 3 - 4 from below:**
- ½ cup shredded carrots
- ½ cup purple cabbage, thinly sliced
- ½ cup cucumber, sliced
- ½ avocado, sliced or cubed
- ½ bell pepper, chopped
- Handful of cherry tomatoes, halved
- Handful of leafy greens (spinach, arugula, or baby kale)
- A few radish slices (optional for extra crunch)

**Protein Options.** (Only light prep needed)
- ½ cup canned chickpeas (rinsed and drained)
- OR ½ cup canned black beans or lentils
- OR ½ block of firm tofu or haloumi, cubed and pan-seared
- OR boiled eggs

**Toppings & Crunch**
- 1 tbsp sesame seeds, sunflower seeds, and/or pumpkin seeds
- 1 tbsp Greek yogurt
- Sprouts, microgreens (really easy to grow)
- Crushed nuts

**Dressing - Lemon Tahini Dressing**

- 2 tbsp tahini
- 1 tbsp lemon juice
- 1 tsp date syrup or honey
- 1 - 2 tbsp water (to thin)
- Pinch of salt and garlic powder (optional)

Mix until smooth and drizzle generously.

**Assembly**

1. Layer the base.
2. Arrange the veggies artfully in sections.
3. Add protein in the centre.
4. Sprinkle seeds and toppings.
5. Drizzle with dressing.

*Create your own recipes*

**What's Actually in My Kitchen?**

Take a few moments to explore your current relationship with food.
This isn't about judgment, it's just about noticing.

**What's in My Cupboard Right Now?**

Make a quick list of eight things from your pantry, fridge, or freezer:

1 ________________________________________

2 ________________________________________

3 ________________________________________

4 ________________________________________

5 ________________________________________

6 ________________________________________

7 ________________________________________

8 ________________________________________

**Now read the ingredients.**

**When I read the ingredient labels on these, I feel:**

🟢 Calm - I know what these things are
🟡 Confused - I recognize some of it, but not all
🔴 A little shocked - There's stuff in here I didn't realize

**What I Know Now:**

After reading this chapter, one thing I want to be more aware of and learn more about is:

--------------------------------------------------------------

--------------------------------------------------------------

--------------------------------------------------------------

--------------------------------------------------------------

**One Small Step I Can Take This Week:**

☐ Check labels before I buy
☐ Prep one real-food snack in advance
☐ Try a new vegetable
☐ Replace one packaged item with a fresh one
☐ Other: _________________________________________

**Affirmation:** *"I don't have to be perfect. I just have to start."*

# Chapter Three: Juices and Smoothies

Liquids are one of the quickest, easiest, and tastiest ways to flood your body with healing nutrients, antioxidants, and hydration.

During a period of intense medical treatment and recovery, juicing became indispensable, first to rebuild strength, later to sustain detoxification and nourishment. I spent countless hours researching healing protocols, eventually blending elements from the Gerson Method, known for its detoxifying raw juices, and the Budwig Protocol, which emphasises flaxseed oil and cottage cheese. The goal was simple: flood the body with restorative nutrients and help bring it back into balance.

Even with a hormone linked breast cancer diagnosis the focus stayed fixed on healing rather than the specifics of chemotherapy, radiation or medication. Daily juicing became a lifeline, a tangible counterbalance to the brutality of treatment. Early on, concerns about sugar shifted the emphasis toward vegetable based combinations, with recipes still evolving through experimentation and nutritional study, even today.

As strength returned, smoothies entered the rotation, offering broader variety plus the critical fibre, nuts, and seeds that juices lacked. Though no longer a daily ritual, both still remain weekly staples. Mornings still pose a challenge as early starts often demand quick solutions. A portable smoothie maker, prepped the night before, easily bridges the gap with minimal effort.

## Types of Juicing

There are three main types of juicers, each with its own strengths and limitations.

| Juicer Type | Pros | Cons | Best For |
|---|---|---|---|
| **Centrifugal** | Fast, affordable | Low yield, heat may destroy nutrients | Beginners |
| **Cold Press** | Nutrient-rich, better for greens | Slower, pricier | Healing and detox |
| **Twin Gear** | Highest quality juice | Expensive, complex | Serious health routines |

## Juicing on a Budget

You don't need an expensive juicer to start. Even a simple blender and strainer can work in the beginning. Prioritise consistency over perfection.

## Juicing vs. Smoothies: Benefits and Considerations

Juicing involves extracting the liquid from fruit and vegetables, leaving behind the fibre. This provides a concentrated dose of vitamins, minerals, and antioxidants that are quickly absorbed into the body. Juices are especially hydrating and nutrient-rich.

However, since the fibre is removed, juices are often digested quickly and may not keep you feeling full for long.

Smoothies are made by blending fruit, vegetables, and other ingredients like yogurt, nuts and seeds, keeping the fibre intact.

This makes smoothies more filling and supportive of digestive health. They're also versatile and easy to adapt based on your cravings or nutritional needs. Smoothies are a great way to mask the flavour of less tasty supplements. I often add ashwagandha or collagen, and they're barely noticeable.

**Things to Keep in Mind**

- Without fibre, juices digest quickly and don't keep you full for long.
- The leftover pulp in juicing may feel wasteful, though it can be repurposed in recipes or for composting.
- Smoothies can be calorie dense, however depending on ingredients can also be energy packed.
- Both juices and smoothies can be high in sugar, specially fruit-heavy drinks which can spike sugar levels. Balance is important.

## The Benefits of Fruit, Vegetables, Nuts, Seeds, and Dates

The magic of smoothies and juices lie in the ingredients. Each food adds its own healing, energising properties, and combining them in colourful ways brings both pleasure and nourishment.

### Fruit & Vegetables by Colour

| Colour | Product | Benefits |
| --- | --- | --- |
| **Red** | Strawberries, cherries, tomatoes | Antioxidants that support the heart and reduce inflammation. |
| **Orange/ Yellow** | Carrots, oranges, mangoes | Vitamin C and beta-carotene, support immune health and vision |
| **Green** | Spinach, kale, cucumber | Detoxifying, rich in iron, magnesium, and chlorophyll. |
| **Blue/ Purple** | Blueberries, purple cabbage | Brain-boosting anthocyanins and anti-aging antioxidants. |
| **White** | Bananas, garlic, cauliflower | Supports digestion, immune function, and heart health. |

## Seeds

Adding nuts and seeds to smoothies is a simple way to boost nutrition and make them more satisfying and filling. They provide healthy fats, plant based protein, fibre, and essential minerals like magnesium and zinc. Blended into your smoothie, ingredients like chia seeds, flaxseeds, almonds, or cashews help support energy, hormone balance, and brain health, while giving your drink a creamy texture and a subtle nutty flavour.

| Seed | Benefits |
| --- | --- |
| **Sunflower Seeds** | Contains Vitamin E, Selenium, Magnesium, Phytosterols. <br> Antioxidant support, reduces inflammation, supports skin and heart health. Aids sleep. |
| **Flax Seeds** | Omega-3s and fibre. <br> Hormonal balance, improves digestion, <br> heart health, reduces cholesterol |
| **Black Seed (Nigella Sativa)** | Immune boosting, anti-inflammatory, <br> supports respiratory and gut health. |
| **Basil Seeds** | Fibre rich and soothing for digestion. <br> Cooling, anti-inflammatory, supports digestion, blood sugar control. <br> Also good for skin. |
| **Pumpkin Seeds** | Contains Zinc, Magnesium, Phytosterols, Tryptophan. <br> Good for prostate health, sleep support, mood regulation, bone and heart health |
| **Chia Seeds** | Omega 3 fatty acids, Fibre, Antioxidants, Protein, all 9 amino acids. <br> Boosts energy, supports digestion, heart health, stabilizes blood sugar, keeps you fuller longer, packed with minerals. |

## Dates

Throwing a couple of dates into your smoothie is an easy, natural way to sweeten it up and give it a nutritional boost and they are packed with fibre, antioxidants, and important minerals like potassium, magnesium, and iron.

Dates blend in beautifully, adding a caramel like sweetness without the crash of refined sugar. Just one or two can balance out bitter greens or strong supplements while supporting digestion, brain health, and blood pressure.

But dates aren't just tasty, they're also great for your health:
- They help your digestion and gut
- Have anti-inflammatory and antioxidant benefits
- Can help keep your blood pressure in check
- Support brain health and memory

Dates are kind of like nature's superfood, almost like honey.

They're so nutrient rich that people have survived on just dates alone for long stretches. Loaded with natural sugars, fibre, and essential minerals, they give you a quick energy hit but also keep you full for longer. That's why dates make such an awesome, wholesome sweetener in smoothies.

Good for your energy and good for your body.

Another unlikely superstar?  Aloe vera.

**Amazing Aloe**

Aloe vera is an incredible plant packed with health boosting benefits, from soothing digestion and supporting gut health to promoting clear skin and reducing inflammation. Its natural compounds and antioxidants, help strengthen the immune system, aid detoxification, and possibly even support blood sugar regulation.

Though aloe's gel can taste quite bitter or earthy on its own, it blends beautifully into smoothies, especially when combined with fruit like pineapple, mango, or berries, making it easy to enjoy its benefits without the aftertaste.

To get fresh aloe gel, simply cut a thick leaf from the base of the plant, slice it open lengthwise, and scoop out the clear inner gel with a spoon. Once extracted, store the gel in an airtight container in the fridge for five to seven days. For longer use, you can also freeze it in ice cube trays for easy, portioned smoothie boosts.

 **Juicing & Smoothies Journal Entry**

This journal invites you to tune into how juices and smoothies make you feel and how they can best serve your unique needs. This is your space for intuitive discovery: no rules, just gentle reflection.

**My Current Relationship With Juicing & Smoothies**

**How do I currently use juices or smoothies in my routine?** (e.g., morning boost, meal replacement, post workout, etc.)

___________________________________________

___________________________________________

**What benefits have I noticed?** (e.g., increased energy, clearer skin, better digestion)

___________________________________________

___________________________________________

**What challenges have I encountered?** (e.g., time, digestion issues, sugar spikes)

___________________________________________

___________________________________________

**After drinking juices or smoothies, I usually feel:**

☐ Energised
☐ Satisfied
☐ Bloated
☐ Thirsty
☐ Refreshed
☐ Sluggish
☐ Clear headed
☐ Hungry again soon

*When do I feel my best or worst after consuming them?* Consider the time of day, what ingredients you used, or what else you consumed.)

_______________________________________________

_______________________________________________

*What cravings or nutritional gaps do I notice?* (E.g., craving salty foods? Still hungry? Need more protein or healthy fat?)

_______________________________________________

_______________________________________________

**Have I Explored the Benefits of Ingredients?** Have I looked into the healing properties of common smoothie/juice add-ins?

☐ Yes
☐ No
☐ Curious to explore more

**Food as Medicine: Which ingredients do I already enjoy using or would like to try?**
☐ Fruit
☐ Vegetables
☐ Seeds
☐ Nuts
☐ Dates
☐ Herbs

*Ingredients I'd love to learn more about:*

_______________________________________________

_______________________________________________

**Recipe Blends for Juices and Smoothies**

**General Instructions for Juices**

1. Use a juicer or blend and strain.
2. Stir well. Taste and adjust (lemon, ginger, or apple can help balance strong flavours).
3. Drink fresh! Juice oxidizes quickly, so consume within 15-30 minutes.

**Juice Blends:**

- **Acne / Skin:** Carrot, Apple, Cucumber, Lemon, Turmeric
- **Anti-Inflammatory:** Turmeric, Pineapple, Ginger, Carrot
- **Anxiety:** Cucumber, Celery, Green Apple, Chamomile
- **Brain Fog / Mental Clarity:** Blueberries, Beetroot, Lemon, Green Tea (cooled)
- **Cold & Flu:** Orange, Lemon, Ginger, Turmeric, Carrot
- **Constipation Relief:** Pear, Prune, Apple, Lemon
- **Detox & Alkalizing:** Spinach, Cucumber, Green Apple, Celery, Lemon
- **Fatigue / Low Energy:** Spinach, Beetroot, Apple, Lemon,
- **Fever Relief:** Watermelon, Mint, Cucumber, Lime
- **Gas & Bloating:** Fennel, Ginger, Green Apple, Mint
- **Hangover Help:** Coconut Water, Cucumber, Ginger, Pineapple, Mint
- **Headache Relief:** Cucumber, Celery, Apple, Mint, Ginger
- **Immune Booster:** Pineapple, Lemon, Ginger, Kale, Apple
- **Liver Cleanse:** Beetroot, Carrot, Lemon, Parsley, Apple
- **Heart Health:** Pomegranate, Red Grapes, Beetroot, Apple
- **PMS / Cramps:** Pineapple, Ginger, Carrot, Parsley
- **Sinus Congestion:** Ginger, Pineapple, Orang
- **Sleep Support:** Cherry, Chamomile Tea (cooled), Banana, Almond Milk
- **Upset Stomach / Indigestion:** Ginger, Apple, Mint, Chamomile
- **Water Retention / Bloating:** Cucumber, Watermelon, Mint, Lemon

**Tip:** Don't discard the froth! While it may separate to the top, it often contains some of the most nutrient dense parts of the juice, packed with enzymes, antioxidants, and fine plant fibres that support digestion and cellular health.

**Create your own recipe:**

**How did I feel afterwards?** *Instant Energy, Hydrated and Renewed, Light and Cleansed*

**How does it support my body?**

Deep Detox  Power  Alkalizing  Brain Fuel  Heart

**General Instructions for Smoothies**

1.  Blend all ingredients until creamy.
2.  Add water, coconut water, or nut milk to adjust thickness.
3.  For best digestion, sip slowly and avoid gulping.

**Smoothie Blends Ideas:**

- **Anxiety / Stress Support**. Banana, Blueberries, Almond Butter, Spinach, Chamomile Tea (cooled)
- **Bloating Relief**. Pineapple, Mint, Cucumber, Coconut Water, Ginger
- **Bone Health**: Kale, Almond Milk, Chia Seeds, Banana, Figs
- **Blood Sugar Balance**: Avocado, Spinach, Blueberries, Flax Seeds, Cinnamon
- **Cardiovascular Support**: Strawberries, Beetroot, Oats, Banana, Almond Milk
- **Energy Boost**: Banana, Dates, Peanuts, Cacao Powder, Oat Milk
- **Insomnia / Sleep Support**: Cherries, Banana, Oats, Almond Milk, Nutmeg
- **Inflammation Relief**: Pineapple, Turmeric, Mango, Ginger, Coconut Water
- **Liver Support**: Dandelion Greens, Lemon, Apple, Cucumber, Coconut Water
- **Immune System Boost**: Orange, Carrot, Ginger, Yogurt or Coconut Yogurt, Honey
- **Mental Clarity / Focus**: Blueberries, Avocado, Walnuts, Coconut Milk, Maca Powder
- **PMS & Hormone Balance**: Berries, Flax Seeds, Almond Butter, Spinach, Plant-Based Milk
- **Post-Workout Recovery**: Banana, Berries, Coconut Water, Chia Seeds
- **Skin / Acne Support**: Carrot, Mango, Lemon, Spinach, Turmeric, Coconut Water
- **Water Retention / Detox**: Watermelon, Mint, Lime, Cucumber, Aloe Vera Juice (optional)

## All-in-One Breakfast Smoothie Recipe

Keeps you full and energised. This blend is packed with fibre, healthy fats, and protein to carry you through the morning.

**Ingredients:**
- ½ cup leftover herbal tea (hibiscus, peppermint, or nettle work well)
- ½ cup Greek or plant-based yogurt
- 1 tbsp each of sunflower, flax, pumpkin, chia, and optional black & basil seeds
- ½ frozen banana
- ½ cup mixed berries
- ½ cup spinach or kale
- tbsp of aloe vera gel
- 1 - 2 dates

## Super Smoothie Bowl

Perfect for days when you want to eat your smoothie with a spoon.

**Ingredients:**
*Frozen berries · Banana · Greek or coconut yogurt · Chia seeds · Flaxseed · Spinach*

**Top With:**
*Granola · Sliced fruit · Coconut flakes · Cacao nibs · Hemp seeds*

## Customisable Bases

**Base Liquids:**
Water · Coconut Water · Herbal Teas (cooled) · Kefir · nut milk - Almond/Oat/Cashew Milk

**Boosters:**
Flaxseed Oil · Aloe Vera Gel · Collagen Powder · Ashwagandha · Maca · Spirulina

**Sweeteners (optional):**
Dates · Raw Honey · Stevia Leaf · Banana

## Smoothie & Juice Rituals

- Freeze chopped fruit in bags for quick grab-and-blend options.
- Prep herbal tea cubes (peppermint, chamomile) to use as a base.
- Keep a smoothie journal - track how you feel before and after.

**Create Your Own Recipe**

*New smoothie combination I'm going to try:*

*How did I feel after drinking my new smoothie recipe?*

*Energised, Light & Refreshed, Mental Clarity, Digestively Happy* - No bloating or discomfort?

_______________________________________________

_______________________________________________

*How does it support my body?*

**Immunity Boost** - Packed with vitamin C from pineapple & lime
**Hydrated** - Cucumber + coconut water replenish electrolytes
**Gut-Friendly** - Pineapple's bromelain + ginger aid digestion
**Alkalizing** - Greens & apple help balance pH

_______________________________________________

_______________________________________________

**Seeds & Nuts: My Nutritional Powerhouses**: *What do I already love using?*

☐ Sunflower
☐ Flax
☐ Pumpkin
☐ Black Seed
☐ Basil Seed
☐ Almonds
☐ Walnuts
☐ Chia

🌰 **Fun fact:** Just *one or two* Brazil nuts a day give you all the selenium your body needs! This mighty mineral keeps your thyroid happy, boosts your immune system, helps fight oxidative stress, and even supports DNA repair. But here's the catch. Too much selenium can backfire, so stick to 1-2 nuts max.

Isn't it amazing how nature packs such powerful benefits into something so small? Mother Earth really knows what she's doing!

**Creating a Routine**

*How can I make smoothies/juices a consistent part of my day?*

_______________________________________________

_______________________________________________

*What combinations get me excited in the morning?*

_______________________________________________

_______________________________________________

*How can I prepare ahead (e.g., freezing fruit, herbal tea cubes)?*

_______________________________________________

_______________________________________________

**Gentle Intentions:** *One small upgrade I can make:*

___________________________________________

___________________________________________

**Interesting Things to Know...**

## 🍭 How Sugar Helps Detect Cancer

Here's something really fascinating from the world of medical diagnostics. When doctors want to locate cancer in the body, they often use something called a **PET scan**.

They inject a tiny amount of radioactive glucose (sugar!) into the bloodstream. Why? Because cancer cells are sugar-hungry and they gobble up glucose way faster than healthy cells. So on the scan, the spots where the sugar collects quickly light up, showing areas where cancer cells might be growing.

In short, cancer cells love sugar and race to it first, and that's how doctors spot them.

Just more proof that what we eat (and what eats us!) matters more than we think. Keep asking questions,  keep your inner detective alive and watch that sugar intake!

**Final Reflection**

This journey isn't about perfection. It's about nourishing yourself with joy, curiosity, and trust. Let your blender become a tool of self-care, one sip at a time.

# Chapter Four: Soups & Broths Healing Nourishment

Across cultures and continents, broths have always been a form of medicine, simple, warm, and deeply nourishing. Whether it's a slow simmered Chinese medicinal bone broth infused with herbs like ginger and goji berries, a fiery West African pepper soup loaded with immune supporting spices, or the gentle, grounding comfort of Ayurvedic *kitchari* made with lentils, rice, and healing spices, these warm, soulful bowls have comforted and restored us for generations.

Often passed down through grandmothers, healers, and community traditions, these recipes were more than just food, they were rituals of care. The warmth supports digestion, the herbs and spices fight inflammation, and the act of sipping slowly invites rest and presence.

In times of illness, stress, or transition, many cultures instinctively turn to broth, not just for physical healing, but for emotional reassurance. A bowl of broth says: *you're safe, you're supported, you're healing.*

Whether you're making a mineral rich veggie broth or a protein-packed bone base, you're participating in an ancient, universal act of nourishment, one sip at a time.

When we're sick, tired, or stressed, our digestion slows. Our nervous system shifts into a protective state. Warm, soft foods are easier to digest and signal safety to the body. In that state of calm, healing becomes possible.

When your body needs a break, a bowl of soup or slow-cooked broth can be pure medicine, gentle, warm, and packed with easily absorbed nutrients. These healing meals nourish you from the inside out.

Broths are nutritional powerhouses, slowly releasing collagen, minerals, and amino acids that support gut repair, reduce inflammation, and enhance immune function. Slow simmering, ideally for 12 to 24 hours, draws these nutrients gently from bones without breaking them down too quickly.

For a quicker alternative, pressure cooking retains much of this nourishment while cutting cooking time dramatically. The high pressure steam helps extract nutrients efficiently, making it an ideal choice when you want healing food without the wait.

**Benefits of pressure cooking include:**

- Retains more nutrients than boiling or frying
- Locks in rich flavours and juices
- Requires minimal oil or water
- Softens tough ingredients like beans and bones for easier digestion
- Keeps your meals wholesome, easy to digest, and nutrient-dense

**Plus, cleanup is minimal with just one pot.**

## Soup as Medicine

Soup isn't just comfort food, it's purposeful nourishment. When we pair the healing properties of specific foods and spices with what our bodies are going through, we begin to eat with intention.

| Symptom | Healing Soup Ideas |
| --- | --- |
| Cold/Flu | Chicken broth with garlic, ginger, turmeric |
| Stomach upset | Plain veggie broth with fennel and cumin |
| Exhaustion | Bone broth with ghee and a pinch of sea salt |
| Inflammation | Red lentil soup with turmeric and cinnamon |
| Anxiety | Ginger, Carrot and Turmeric |

## Key Benefits of Bone Broth

That said, if you're making a proper **bone broth**, slow and steady is still best. The longer you cook it, the more goodness gets pulled out of the bones and into the broth.

We're talking about things like:

**Collagen**, which turns into gelatine and helps with joint health, skin, hair, nails, and even gut healing.

**Minerals** like calcium, magnesium, and phosphorus, which are released slowly and need time to really infuse the broth.

**Amino acids** like glycine and proline, which support the liver, reduce inflammation, and help your body repair itself.

Bones are tough. They're literally made to support bodies, so they take time to break down. A quick boil just won't do it. Slow simmering over hours gently draws out all those nutrients without destroying them.

61

**What role do soups or broths currently play in your diet?**
☐ Comfort food
☐ Easy go-to
☐ Rarely eat them
☐ Healing ritual
☐ Trying to add more
☐ I'm curious to experiment

*When was the last time a simple meal made you feel truly nourished, body and soul?*

_______________________________________________

_______________________________________________

*What do you notice about your digestion, energy, or mood after eating warm, soft meals like soup or broth?*

_______________________________________________

_______________________________________________

*Are there ingredients you find especially comforting or healing?*

☐   Spices (like turmeric, ginger)?
☐   Herbs (parsley, coriander)?
☐   Roots (carrots, garlic)?
☐   Broth base (bone or veggie)?

_______________________________________________

_______________________________________________

*What small upgrade could you make this week?*
☐ Prep broth in advance
☐ Try pressure cooking
☐ Add healing herbs
☐ Replace 1 meal with a soup

_______________________________________________

_______________________________________________

## Instant Pot Mixed Veg Soup
(Comforting, nourishing & simple even if you don't like cooking)

**Base Flavours (Sauté in Instant Pot using Sauté Mode, 3 - 5 min):**
- 1 tbsp olive oil or ghee
- 1 onion, chopped
- 2 garlic cloves, minced
- 1-inch ginger, minced (optional)

**Vegetables (Choose 4 - 5):**
- 1 carrot, diced
- 1 cup cauliflower florets
- 1 cup chopped green beans
- 1 zucchini, sliced
- 1 cup shredded cabbage
- ½ bell pepper, chopped
- 1 tomato, chopped
- Handful of spinach or kale (stir in after cooking)

**Additions:** • ½ cup red lentils OR ½ cup cooked brown rice or quinoa (for heartiness)
- 4 cups vegetable broth or water
- ½ tsp turmeric
- Salt and pepper to taste

**Finishing Touches:** • Fresh lemon juice (1 tbsp)
- Fresh parsley or coriander to serve
- Drizzle of olive oil or spoon of yogurt on top (optional)

**Instructions:**
- Sauté onion, garlic, and ginger in oil until softened.
- Add your chosen veggies and lentils/grains.
- Pour in broth, add spices.
- Close lid, cook on High Pressure for 6 - 8 minutes.

Quick or natural release. Stir in leafy greens and lemon juice.
Taste and adjust seasoning. Serve hot, topped with fresh herbs.

## Healing Broth (Basic Bone or Veggie-Based)

**If you're using bones (for bone broth):**
- 1 kg (2 lbs) bones: chicken, beef, lamb or fish (preferably with joints and marrow)
- 1 tablespoon apple cider vinegar (helps pull minerals from the bones)

**For veggie version:**
- 2 large carrots, chopped
- 2 celery sticks, chopped
- 1 onion, quartered
- 4 - 5 garlic cloves, smashed
- A thumb-sized piece of ginger, sliced
- A small handful of parsley or coriander
- 1 teaspoon turmeric (fresh or powder)
- 1 bay leaf
- A pinch of sea salt
- Black pepper to taste
- Optional: a piece of seaweed for extra minerals
- 8 - 10 cups filtered water

**Method:**

**If using a pot (slow and steady):**

1. Add everything to a large pot.
2. Bring to a gentle boil, then turn the heat right down.
3. Let it simmer on very low for:
   - **Veggie broth**: 1.5 to 2 hours
   - **Bone broth**: minimum 8 hours, ideally 12 - 24 hours
4. Skim off any foam that comes to the top in the first hour.
5. Strain and sip! Store in the fridge for up to 5 days or freeze in batches.

**If using a pressure cooker / Instant Pot:**

- Add all ingredients to the pot.
- Set to high pressure for:
- **Veggie broth**: 30 - 40 minutes
- **Bone broth**: 90 minutes to 2 hours
- Let pressure release naturally. Then strain and enjoy!

## Cold or Flu - Chicken Broth with Garlic, Ginger & Turmeric

A warming, immune boosting soup that fights infection and soothes congestion.

**Ingredients:**
- 1 tbsp olive oil or ghee
- 1 small onion, chopped
- 3 garlic cloves, smashed
- 1-inch piece of ginger, sliced
- ½ tsp ground turmeric (or 1-inch fresh)
- 1 carrot, chopped
- 1 celery stalk, chopped
- 2 - 3 cups chicken bone broth
- Salt and pepper to taste
- Juice of ½ lemon (optional)

**Instructions:**

1. In a pot, heat oil and sauté onion, garlic, and ginger until fragrant.
2. Add turmeric, carrot, and celery. Stir for 2 minutes.
3. Pour in broth. Simmer for 15 - 20 minutes.
4. Add salt, pepper, and lemon juice if desired. Sip slowly.

## Stomach Upset - Plain Veggie Broth with Fennel & Cumin

Gentle and soothing for nausea, cramps, or bloating.

### Ingredients:

- 1 tsp olive oil
- 1 small fennel bulb or 1 tsp fennel seeds
- ½ tsp cumin seeds
- 1 carrot, chopped
- 1 small potato, peeled and chopped
- 1 bay leaf
- 4 cups water
- Pinch of salt

### Instructions:

1. Heat oil in a pot, lightly toast cumin and fennel seeds.
2. Add veggies and bay leaf, stir for 2 - 3 minutes.
3. Add water and salt, bring to a boil, then reduce to simmer for 30 minutes.
4. Strain and sip the broth, or puree for a light soup.

## Exhaustion - Bone Broth with Ghee & Sea Salt

Replenishing, grounding, and deeply mineralizing.

### Ingredients:

- 2 - 3 cups bone broth (chicken, beef, or lamb)
- 1 tsp ghee (clarified butter)
- A pinch of high quality sea salt
- Optional: pinch of ashwagandha powder for adrenal support

### Instructions:

1. Warm bone broth on the stove.
2. Stir in ghee and salt.
3. Add ashwagandha if using.
4. Pour into a mug and sip slowly like a tonic.

## Inflammation - Red Lentil Soup with Turmeric & Cinnamon

Anti-inflammatory and blood sugar balancing.

**Ingredients:**
- 1 tbsp olive oil or coconut oil
- 1 small onion, chopped
- 2 garlic cloves, minced
- ½ tsp turmeric
- ¼ tsp cinnamon
- 1 cup red lentils, rinsed
- 4 cups water or vegetable broth
- Salt and pepper to taste
- Optional: squeeze of lemon or a dollop of yogurt

**Instructions:**

1. Heat oil and sauté onion and garlic.
2. Add turmeric and cinnamon; stir briefly.
3. Add lentils and liquid. Simmer 20 - 25 minutes.
4. Season and blend (optional) for a creamy texture.

## Anxiety - Ginger, Carrot & Turmeric Soup

Grounding, warming, and soothing for the nervous system.

**Ingredients:**
- 1 tbsp ghee or olive oil
- 1 onion, chopped
- 2 garlic cloves, minced
- 1-inch ginger, grated
- ½ tsp turmeric
- 4 large carrots, chopped
- 3 cups vegetable broth
- Salt to taste
- Optional: fresh parsley or coriander to serve

**Instructions:**

1.  Sauté onion, garlic, and ginger in ghee/oil.
2.  Add turmeric and carrots; stir to coat.
3.  Pour in broth and simmer for 20 minutes.
4.  Blend until smooth. Top with fresh herbs and breathe deeply.

**What's your go-to healing soup idea?** *Try building your own recipe from what's already in your kitchen. (Hint: Use the veggie base, a grain or pulse, a warming spice, and fresh herbs!)*

🛠 **Healing Toolkit Check-In:**
*Have I stocked my freezer or fridge with broth for when I'm tired or unwell?*

___________________________________________

___________________________________________

*Do I have a pressure cooker or Instant Pot, and am I using it to make life easier*

___________________________________________

___________________________________________

*Could I create a "Soup Sunday" ritual for calm, prep, and nourishment?*

___________________________________________

___________________________________________

When life feels heavy or your body needs rest, a bowl of soup or healing broth can remind you of something deeper, that nourishment can be simple. That healing doesn't always need to come in a bottle or a lab. That you can hold wellness in your hands, one spoonful at a time.

The recipes in this chapter aren't just comfort food. They are nourishment with intention. Liquid resilience. They're here to remind your body that healing is possible, and that even on the hardest days, warmth can return.

And while broths and soups provide a beautiful base for recovery, much of their power comes from what's infused into them, the *herbs and spices* that carry ancient wisdom, bold flavours, and therapeutic strength. These little leaves, roots, and seeds have worked alongside us for centuries: calming our nerves, soothing our digestion, fortifying our immunity, and adding soul to our cooking.

So now, let's open the next chapter, and unlock the healing magic of herbs and spice.

# Chapter Five:  The Healing Magic of Herbs and Spice

Just like my journey with food, juicing, and smoothies, herbs came into my life naturally, almost as if they were quietly waiting for me to notice them. The deeper I went into wellness, the more they revealed themselves.

At first, I tossed a few into my juices, then into meals. Soon, I was brewing herbal teas and experimenting with healing blends. The more I read and watched, stories of people using herbs to manage everything from minor ailments to chronic illnesses like cancer, the more I realised the immense power locked inside these humble plants, many of them considered weeds.

Each herb is a world of its own. From roots and bark to leaves and flowers, they're made up  of trillions of compounds, many with potent healing properties. Of course, not all herbs are friendly to the human body, so respect and knowledge are key.

But when understood and used wisely, herbs become more than just ingredients. They become allies; gentle, grounding, and deeply supportive across the physical, emotional, and spiritual planes.

Herbs and spices can be woven into your life in countless ways: simmered into nourishing meals, steeped as calming teas, infused into potent tinctures, massaged in balms, chewed and even eaten fresh from the garden. Their versatility is both ancient and limitless.

In this chapter, we'll look at how you can bring herbs and spices into your daily routine, through simple teas, tasty recipes, and powerful remedies like tinctures and salves. By the end, you'll have many ways to use the healing energy of plants in your life.

From common cooking herbs to fruit, oils and roots, your kitchen is a pharmacy of healing. Before the rise of pharmaceuticals, people relied entirely on what the earth provided. In fact, many of today's drugs are derived from nature and then altered for patenting.

**Here are just a few natural products with powerful medicinal properties:**

- **Cayenne Pepper** - Boosts circulation, relieves pain, heart protective
- **Chamomile** - Calming, sleep aid, digestive support
- **Coconut Oil** - Antifungal, brain health, skin and hair nourishment
- **Honey** - Antibacterial, wound healing, soothes coughs
- **Garlic** - Antimicrobial, supports heart and immune health
- **Ginger** - Anti-nausea, supports digestion, Anti-inflammatory
- **Liquorice Root** - Soothes digestion, cough, and adrenal support
- **Lemon** - Alkalising, supports liver detox and immunity
- **Mint** - Soothes digestion, headaches, and respiratory issues
- **Nettle** - High in iron, supports kidney function and reduces inflammation
- **Sunlight (Vitamin D)** - Bone health, immunity, mood regulation
- **Willow Bark** - Natural pain relief and Anti-inflammatory (the original aspirin)

🖊 *Which of these natural medicines have you used, or are curious to try?*

_______________________________________________

_______________________________________________

*What do you already have in your kitchen that might double as healing?*

_______________________________________________

_______________________________________________

**Why It Makes Sense to Begin with What You Need**

I chose to begin introducing the uses of herbs, rather than listing individual herbs and their specific properties, for two key reasons:

- **First,** many common ailments can be addressed with herbs and spices you likely *already have in your kitchen*. There's often no need to rush out and buy herbs right away.
- **Second,** there are more than 28,000 medicinal herbs known worldwide. So finding a starting point can be overwhelming.

That's why it often makes more sense to begin with your need, what you want to support or heal, and then match the herbs to that.

When I first began exploring herbal remedies, my cupboards were overflowing with containers labelled with each herb's benefits, nutrients, and instructions for use.

Over time, I've simplified my approach and now focus on **a smaller, targeted collection** of herbs chosen for specific purposes.

🌿 **Everyday Herbs & Spices: Nature's Kitchen Pharmacy**

Not everyone has the means or interest in buying specific herbs, so we are first going to focus on herbs and spices that you probably already have in your kitchen.

**Let's start with the astonishing benefits of these amazing staples.**

**Basil**: Anti-inflammatory | Promotes liver detox | Calms stress | Supports immune system | Aids digestion | Heart & circulation health | Energy booster

**Cilantro (Coriander):** Detoxes heavy metals | Antioxidant | Anti-inflammatory | Supports liver | Aids digestion | Boosts immunity | Regulates blood sugar & cholesterol

**Dill:** Anti-inflammatory | Antioxidant | Antibacterial Aids digestion | Blood sugar regulation | Bone support Immune booster | Promotes sleep

**Mint:** Anti-inflammatory | Antioxidant | Eases digestion | Soothes headaches & nausea | Eases respiratory issues | Oral health | Boosts energy & focus | 🏋Relieves muscle pain | Skin support

**Oregano:** Antibacterial | Antioxidant | Antifungal | Gut & immune support | Supports respiratory system

**Parsley:** High in vitamin K, iron, folate, chlorophyll | Aids detox & kidney function | Heart & circulation health | Hormone balance | Freshens breath

**Rosemary:** Antioxidant-rich | Supports memory | Aids digestion | Boosts circulation | Encourages hair growth | Elevates mood | Reduces stress | Boosts energy

**Sage**: Antioxidant | Anti-inflammatory | Antimicrobial Enhances cognition | Balances blood sugar | Relieves menopause symptoms | Improves mood | Supports skin health

**Thyme**: Antiseptic | Strengthens immunity | Supports respiratory health | Aids digestion

**Other Pantry Heroes**

**Allspice**: Anti-inflammatory | Antioxidant | Antimicrobial | Aids digestion | Relieves pain | Supports circulation | Eases cold & flu symptoms

**Apple Cider Vinegar**: Balances blood sugar |Supports gut health | Antimicrobial | Heart health | Balances body pH | Detoxifying | Skin support

**Black Pepper**: Enhances nutrient absorption (especially curcumin) | Antioxidant | Anti-inflammatory | Antibacterial | Aids digestion | Boosts metabolism | Improves brain function | Supports respiratory health

**Cardamom**: Antioxidant | Anti-inflammatory | Supports oral health | Lowers blood pressure | Detoxifies the body | Aids respiratory health | Enhances mood

**Cayenne Pepper:** Boosts circulation & metabolism | Pain relief | Aids digestion | Anti-inflammatory | Clears congestion | Antimicrobial

- **Cayenne Pepper's Heart Health Specifics**: Improves circulation, Lowers blood pressure, Reduces bad cholesterol (LDL), Prevents blood clots, Lowers triglycerides

**Cinnamon:** Digestive aid | Anti-inflammatory | Antioxidant | Antimicrobial | Regulates blood sugar | Supports heart health | Boosts brain function |May have anti-cancer effects

**Cloves**: Antioxidant | Anti-inflammatory | Antimicrobial | Supports oral health | Aids digestion | Blood sugar support | Strengthens immunity | Eases respiratory issues

**Garlic**: Immune booster | Lowers blood pressure & cholesterol | Antioxidant | Anti-inflammatory | May help prevent cancer |Supports detox | Aids bone health

**Mustard Seeds:** Antioxidant | Anti-inflammatory | Antibacterial | Supports digestion & gut health | Boosts circulation & heart health | Balances blood sugar | Hormone support | Detoxifying | May support brain health

**Onions:** Antioxidant | Anti-inflammatory | Natural antibiotic | Rich in prebiotics for gut health | Heart health | Immune support |Regulates blood sugar | Bone support | Supports digestion |Potential cancer-fighting properties

**Turmeric (with Black Pepper!)**: Potent Anti-inflammatory | Healing powerhouse | Boosts brain power | Aids digestion | Joint support | Heart health | Manages blood sugar | Immune support | Possible anti-cancer effects

**Key Properties of Natural Foods**

Each of these herbs and spices has extensive benefits, and you'll discover what works best for you through personal experience. *Keep in mind that nearly every fruit and vegetable offers similar advantages.*

**🌿 Plant Compounds with Cancer-Related Potential**

Nature's full of healing power, and it's about time we gave it the credit it deserves. Some plants are already well known for their ability to help the body fight off abnormal cell growth. Dandelion root, for example, is finally being recognised for its ability to target cancer cells while leaving healthy ones alone.

Turmeric, green tea, and a few other natural heroes consistently show up in studies for their protective and healing properties.

While research continues, one thing is clear: the natural world has always had our back and we're just starting to catch up.

**As for me, I believe the reason I'm still here today, sharing this knowledge, is largely thanks to the power of herbs.**

**Why Start with Tea?**

Teas are one of the simplest, easiest ways to incorporate healing herbs and spices into your life. These teas are soothing, hydrating, and packed with nutrients. Plus, they give you the chance to experiment with different herbs and discover what resonates with your body.

Herb shops are on every street corner now, and online providers are abundant.  Do your homework on what you want to achieve and then order your herbs, or just start with the ones in your kitchen.

**Adaptogens - Nature's Stress Relievers**

**Adaptogens are specific herbs that help balance the body and support its natural response to stress.** They regulate hormones, enhance overall health, and promote resilience. Adaptogens work across various organs and systems to strengthen the body and improve its ability to cope with stress and environmental challenges that place it under pressure.

💡**Pro tip:** Include at least one adaptogen in your daily tea or tonic for everyday balance and support.

## Common Adaptogens & Their Benefits

| <u>Herb</u> | <u>Benefits</u> | <u>How to Use</u> |
|---|---|---|
| **Ashwagandha**<br>Taste: Bitter, earthy | Calms anxiety, improves energy, balances hormones. | Mix powder into warm milk (Golden Milk), teas, smoothies, or take in a capsule. |
| **Holy Basil (Tulsi)**<br>Taste: Sweet, slightly spicy | Reduces stress, boosts focus, supports respiratory health. | Brew as tea, add to curries, or infuse into honey. |
| **Liquorice Root**<br>Taste: Sweet, distinct | Soothes the throat, supports liver health, strengthens immunity. | Add to teas or chew a small piece after meals. |
| **Nettle**<br>**Taste:** Earthy, mild | Anti-inflammatory, rich in iron, calcium, magnesium, and vitamins. Supports kidneys, lungs, and digestion | Add to teas, soups, or smoothies. |

**Other Notable Adaptogens:** Astragalus • Basil • Black Pepper • Cardamom Chamomile • Cinnamon • Cloves • Cordyceps • Ginger • Ginseng • Goji Berry • Lavender • Lemon Balm • Maca Root • Moringa • Nutmeg • Passionflower • Reishi Mushrooms • Rhodiola Rosea • Rose (petals & hips) • Rosemary • Saffron • Sage • Thyme • Turmeric

**Let's start by looking at some common ailments that people treat with herbs.**

**For Brain Function & Clarity**
*Focus, memory, clarity. These support mental sharpness and circulation.*
Ginkgo Biloba • Rosemary • Sage • Matcha • Turmeric • Periwinkle • Siberian Ginseng • Moringa • Cayenne Pepper • Black Pepper

**For Endocrine Support (Hormone Balance)**
*These herbs support hormonal harmony and balance over time.*
Ashwagandha • Maca Root • Holy Basil • Ginseng • Liquorice Root Fenugreek • Siberian Ginseng • Black Cohosh • Cinnamon • Parsley • Coriander (Cilantro)

**For Immune Support**
*Protective herbs that fortify your natural defences.*
Echinacea • Astragalus • Elderberry • Garlic • Ginger • Turmeric • Reishi • Shiitake • Olive Leaf • Oregano • Thyme • Liquorice Root • Moringa • Ginseng • Cinnamon • Black Pepper • Cloves • Parsley

**For Stress & Sleep**
*Soothing, grounding, and calming. These herbs help the body unwind.*
Ashwagandha • Holy Basil • Lemon Balm • Chamomile • Lavender • Passionflower • Valerian Root • Reishi • Kava Kava • Cardamom • Nutmeg • Sage • Rosemary

**Willow Bark**

**For Pain Relief**
*Natural pain relievers that reduce inflammation and ease discomfort.*
White Willow Bark • Turmeric • Ginger • Boswellia (Frankincense) • Clove • Cayenne • Arnica • Peppermint • Feverfew • Meadowsweet • Cat's Claw • Arnica • Valerian Root • Chamomile • Hops

**For Headaches & Migraines**
*These herbs target tension, inflammation, and circulation to relieve headaches.*
Peppermint • Willow Bark • Ginger • Lavender • Rosemary • Ginkgo Biloba • Chamomile

**For Stomach Aches & Digestion**
*Soothe the gut, calm spasms, and aid digestive flow.*
Peppermint • Fennel • Ginger • Chamomile • Liquorice Root • Lemon Balm • Angelica Root • Caraway • Dandelion Root • Marshmallow Root

**For Acidity & Reflux**
*Cooling, mucilaginous, and Anti-inflammatory herbs that calm the stomach lining.*
Liquorice Root • Marshmallow Root • Slippery Elm • Aloe Vera Juice • Chamomile • Fennel • Cardamom • Holy Basil • Ginger • Cayenne Pepper

**Heart Health.** If you are worried about your heart and circulation, here are a few ideas to get you started:

- **For Circulation**: *Herbs that improve blood flow and support vascular health.*
  Ginkgo Biloba • Cayenne Pepper • Ginger • Horse Chestnut • Garlic • Rosemary • Gotu Kola
- **For Cholesterol**: *Herbs that help manage cholesterol levels and support heart health.*
  Fenugreek • Garlic • Turmeric • Ginger • Artichoke Leaf • Psyllium Husk • Green Tea • Guggul

- For Blood Pressure: *Herbs that support healthy blood pressure by promoting relaxation and cardiovascular health.*
  Hawthorn • Garlic • Olive Leaf • Hibiscus • Basil • Ginger • Turmeric • Cinnamon • Cayenne Pepper

Based on what I've learned through experience, here are the **non-kitchen herbs** I would recommend starting with:

- **Willow Bark (Nature's Aspirin):** Adaptogen; supports pain relief, anti-inflammatory effects, fever reduction, cramps, joint and bone health, circulation, and cardiovascular health.
- **Nettle:** Adaptogen; helps with allergies, inflammation, detoxification, pain relief, hormone balance, iron and red blood cell production, urinary tract health, blood sugar regulation, digestion, immune support, Skin and hair health.
- **Moringa (the "Miracle Tree"):** Adaptogen and antioxidant; supports anti-inflammatory effects, detoxification, blood sugar control, heart health, immunity, brain function, digestion, and skin and hair care.
- **Liquorice:** Adaptogen; benefits digestion, respiratory health, adrenal support, inflammation, hormone balance, antiviral and antibacterial activity, and liver function.
- **Echinacea:** Adaptogen; boosts immune and respiratory health, reduces inflammation, fights viruses and bacteria, supports skin healing, and helps with anxiety.
- **Hibiscus:** Supports blood pressure regulation, heart health, cholesterol management, antioxidant effects, liver function, weight control, anti-inflammatory and antibacterial benefits, blood sugar control, acts as a diuretic, and provides menstrual support.
- **Mint/Peppermint:** Relieves headaches, nausea, motion sickness, respiratory issues; improves mood and stress, has antiviral and antibacterial properties, supports oral and skin health, and aids IBS symptoms.
- **Lemon Balm (Melissa), Chamomile, or Lavender:** Promotes stress relief and better sleep.

- **Dandelion:** Supports liver health, digestion, acts as a diuretic, reduces inflammation, helps regulate blood sugar, boosts immunity, and supports skin health and cancer prevention.

It's really simple to use these herbs. Just steep them in a pot of hot water and enjoy; hot or cold. If you don't like the taste, feel free to adjust the recipe or add another flavour. I often use hibiscus (or roselle) which has a multitude of benefits and also masks unpleasant flavours. If you prefer something sweeter, add honey or a dash of cinnamon. Many herbs, especially the flowers, have naturally sweet notes.

🍵 **Tea Instructions:**

1.  Pour boiling water over herbs.
2.  Steep for 10 - 15 minutes.
3.  Strain if you want to
4.  Sip warm or cold.

**Example: My Daily Adaptogenic Tea**

I blend my tea with purpose. Here's what I use and why:

- **1 tsp nettle** - an adaptogen that balances the body
- **1 tsp horsetail** - supports bone health
- **1 tsp hawthorn** - strengthens the heart
- **2 - 3 tsp hibiscus (or roselle)** - improves flavour, acts as a diuretic, and supports blood pressure

**Let's look closer at just <u>one</u> herb: The Benefits of Nettle**

1. **Nutrients** include vitamins A, C, K, B-complex; minerals like iron, zinc, calcium, magnesium, and silica
2. **Anti-inflammatory**
3. **Immune boosting**
4. **Urinary health**
5. **Circulation & blood sugar regulation**
6. **Gentle detoxifier**
7. **Skin support**
8. **Hair growth**
9. **Allergies**

It's truly astonishing that something so often dismissed as a weed, like nettle, can offer such a wealth of benefits. In fact most weeds are powerhouses.  Forget grass. Grow weeds!

But that's the magic of plants. Each one holds a multitude of healing properties, and exploring them has become a deeply rewarding journey of discovery.

Every time I learned about a new herb, I felt compelled to seek it out and try it for myself. That curiosity hasn't faded! I'm still learning, still uncovering new plants and their potential.

Over time, though, I've come to understand what works for me and what doesn't. Our bodies are unique, each functioning in its own way. What brings balance and wellness to one person may not have the same effect on another.

Yet for me, there's something quietly powerful about the ritual of making herbal tea. I know, whether it's the herbs themselves or the placebo effect at work, that it's doing something positive.

And in the end, that belief alone is enough. Healing is as much about mindset as it is about method.

**Tea Recipes**

## Lung and Respiration

**Purpose:** Designed to open airways, ease congestion, and support overall respiratory health.

**Ingredients:**
- Ginger - A thin slice *or* 1 tsp ground ginger
- Turmeric - A small piece of fresh root *or* 1 tsp dried turmeric
- 6 - 8 mint leaves
- 2 - 3 eucalyptus leaves

**Tip:** Drink warm to help soothe the chest and promote easier breathing.

## Focus & Mental Energy Blend

**Purpose:** Sharpens focus, enhances alertness, and supports clear thinking. Ideal for study sessions or creative work.

**Ingredients:**
- Rosemary - 1 sprig *or* ½ tsp dried rosemary
- Ginger - A thin slice *or* 1 tsp ground ginger
- A pinch of black pepper (to activate beneficial compounds)

Add to 1 cup of brewed green tea and stew for a few minutes

<u>**Evening Calm Tea**</u> **- For Relaxation & Sleep**

**Purpose:** Encourages a sense of calm and helps ease the mind into restful sleep.

**Ingredients:**
- 1 tsp lemon balm (melissa)
- 1 tsp chamomile flowers
- 1 piece of valerian root *(note: strong smell but very effective)*

Drink 30 minutes before bed.

<u>**Headache Relief Tea**</u>

**Purpose:** Relaxes and helps ease mild headaches.

**Ingredients:**
- Fresh mint (or ½ tsp dried)
- Ginger - A thin slice *or* 1 tsp ground ginger
- Chamomile flowers
- Basil leaves (or ½ tsp dried)

**Tip:** Best served warm and sipped slowly in a calm environment.

<u>**Stomach Ache Soothing Tea**</u>

**Purpose:** Soothes inflammation in the digestive tract and helps reduce acidity.

**Ingredients:**
- 1 tsp crushed fennel seeds
- 1 tsp dried chamomile flowers
- 1 tsp lemon balm (melissa)
- 1 tsp fresh mint leaves
- A slice of fresh ginger *(or 1 tsp of powder)*

## Acidity & Reflux Relief Tea

**Purpose:** Soothes inflammation in the digestive tract and helps reduce acidity.

**Ingredients:**
- 1 stick of marshmallow root
- A few sticks of dried plantain
- A stick of liquorice root
- 1 tsp crushed coriander seeds
- A stick of cinnamon

**Tip:** Drink between meals, not right after eating, to help soothe the digestive lining.

## Period Pain & Cramping

**Ingredients:**
- 1 tsp dried raspberry leaf
- 1 tsp dried chamomile flowers
- 1 piece of ginger (½ tsp powdered ginger)
- Optional: drop of honey for sweetness

## Migraine Relief Tea

**Ingredients:**
- 1 piece of willow bark
- 1 tsp peppermint
- ½ tsp lavender flowers
- Optional: fresh lemon slice

## Hormonal Balance (Endocrine Support) Tea

**Ingredients:**
- 1 tsp fresh or dried holy basil (Tulsi)
- 1 tsp dried ashwagandha root
- 1 piece of  cinnamon or ½ tsp cinnamon
- Optional: ½ tsp liquorice root

## Everyday Balance & Wellness Tea

**Ingredients:**
- 1 tsp dried nettle leaf
- 1 tsp dried lemon balm
- ½ tsp dried rosemary
- Optional: goji berries or fresh mint

## Memory-Boosting Rosemary & Sage Tea

**Ingredients:**
- 1 tsp rosemary
- 1 tsp sage
- 1 tsp honey (optional)

## Stress-Relief Lavender & Rose Tea

**Ingredients:**
- 1 tsp dried lavender
- 1 tsp dried rose petals
- 1 tsp honey (optional)

**Create your own tea blend**

*Write down your blend's purpose (e.g., stress relief, immune support, digestion).*

______________________________________________________

______________________________________________________

*Label it with: name, date created, herbs used, healing intent.*

______________________________________________________

______________________________________________________

*Optional: Design a name for your blend and journal about why you chose it.*

______________________________________________________

______________________________________________________

*Which three herbs or spices in this chapter call to you the most, and why?*

______________________________________________________

______________________________________________________

**Which adaptogen(s) from this chapter would best support you right now?** *Write about how you'd like to incorporate them into your routine.*

_______________________________________________________

_______________________________________________________

*Choose 3 - 5 more herbs that resonate with your current health needs.*

_______________________________________________________

_______________________________________________________

*How does it change your perspective to see everyday ingredients as medicine?*

_______________________________________________________

_______________________________________________________

Herbs aren't just for tea, they're a great way to enhance everyday meals. Fresh, homemade salad dressings are an easy way to bring your herbs to life and make even the simplest greens feel special.

And if you love pesto and mustard but not the price tags or the preservatives, making your own is easy, budget friendly, and deeply satisfying.

# Fresh, Tangy Salad Dressing with Pomegranate Twist

A good dressing can completely transform a simple salad. If you're aiming to eat more greens, this vibrant blend adds flavour, colour, and a touch of natural sweetness.

**Ingredients:**

- 3 tbsp extra virgin olive oil
- 1 tbsp fresh lemon juice *or* apple cider vinegar
- 2 tbsp pomegranate juice (for sweetness and a fruity kick)
- 1 tsp mustard (use your home made mustards and play with the tastes)
- Honey *or* date syrup to taste
- 2 tbsp finely chopped fresh herbs (such as mint, parsley, basil, dill, or watercress)
- 2 tbsp pomegranate seeds (optional, for texture and a burst of flavour)
- Sea salt and freshly ground black pepper, to taste
- *Optional:* 1 small garlic clove, finely minced for added depth

**Method:**
1. Put all ingredients in a small jar or bowl.
2. Shake or whisk until well blended and slightly thickened.
3. Taste and adjust. Add more lemon juice or a bit more juice/honey if you prefer it sweeter.

**Tip:** Store in the fridge for up to 5 days. Shake well before each use as the ingredients may naturally separate.

# Classic Basil Pesto Recipe

A fragrant, creamy pesto that's perfect for pasta, sandwiches, or as a dip!

**Ingredients:**
- 2 cups packed fresh basil leaves
- ½ cup grated Parmesan cheese
- ⅓ cup pine nuts
- 2 - 3 garlic cloves
- ½ cup extra virgin olive oil (plus extra for storage)
- Salt & black pepper

*Optional:* A squeeze of lemon juice

🥣 **Methods:**
1. Heat a dry skillet over medium heat.
2. Add  pine nuts and toast for 2 - 3 minutes, stirring often, until golden and aromatic.
3. Let cool slightly before blending.
4. In a food processor, pulse basil, nuts, garlic, and Parmesan until coarsely chopped.
5. With the processor running, slowly drizzle in olive oil until smooth.
6. For a thinner pesto, add more oil; for thicker, use less.
7. Taste and add salt, pepper, or lemon juice as needed.
8. Keep in an airtight jar in the fridge for up to 1 week. Top with a thin oil layer to prevent browning.
9. Pour into ice cube trays for easy single-use portions!

## 🟡 <u>Simple Homemade Mustard Recipe</u>

Make your own flavourful mustard from scratch with just a few ingredients. Customize it to suit your taste, mild, spicy, sweet, or tangy.

📝 Ingredients:
- ½ cup **mustard seeds** (yellow for milder flavour, brown or black for more heat)
- ½ cup **vinegar** (apple cider or white wine)
- ½ cup **water** (or beer for extra flavour)
- 1 - 2 tsp sea or Himalayan **salt**
- 1 - 2 tsp **honey or date syrup**(optional, for a hint of sweetness)
- Optional: turmeric, garlic powder, chili flakes, or herbs

🥣 Instructions:
- Put whole mustard seeds in a glass container and cover with your liquid base (vinegar-water blend or beer for deeper flavour).
- Secure with a breathable lid or cloth and leave at room temperature for 5-7 days.
- Shake or stir the mixture daily by swirling or stirring gently to develop flavour.
- Transfer the seeds and liquid to your blender.
- Add salt, optional natural sweeteners (like honey or date syrup), and any additional flavour enhancers (garlic, turmeric, etc.).
- Blend to achieve your preferred texture. Quick pulses maintain rustic texture while continuous blending creates a silky finish.
- Conduct a taste test and balance flavours as needed.

Note: Freshly blended mustard will be quite strong initially, but gradually softens over 3-5 days. Store in sterilized jars.

⟳ **Variations:**

- **Dijon-style:** Replace water with dry white wine and add a small clove of garlic during blending.
- **Honey Mustard:** Mix in an extra tablespoon or two of honey for a sweeter twist.
- **Spicy Mustard:** Use a higher ratio of brown or black mustard seeds and add chili flakes or a bit of horseradish for heat.

*Mustard seeds are a common spice in many cultures. How do different cultural foods make you feel? Reflect on a dish that ties into your roots or experiences.*

_______________________________________________

_______________________________________________

*Which herbs or spices do you already use? How can you introduce one new healing option this week?*

_______________________________________________

_______________________________________________

## 💧 Making Tinctures: Concentrated Herbal Remedies

Tinctures are strong herbal medicines made by soaking plants in alcohol, vinegar, or glycerine. They've been used for thousands of years and are still popular today because they're easy to make, last long, and work well.

A great example is **Rescue Remedy**, the famous stress-relief tincture blend. Made from flower essences (like rock rose and cherry plum), it's designed to calm nerves *instantly*. Just a few drops under the tongue can help with panic, stage fright, or shock. Like all tinctures, it's concentrated, portable, and absorbs quicker than tea, making it perfect for emergencies or daily stress.

**A Bit of History**
- Ancient Roots: Egyptians made tinctures in clay pots over 3,000 years ago.
- Traditional Use: Herbalists in Europe and Asia used them to treat everything from colds to pain.
- Still Used Today: Modern herbalists and doctors sometimes recommend them as natural remedies.

## 🌿 How to Make a Simple Tincture
1. Pour your herb into a glass jar or bottle (e.g., rosemary, liquorice, or oregano).
2. Cover with vodka, apple cider vinegar or glycerine.
3. Seal and store in a cool, dark place for 4 - 6 weeks, shaking regularly (usually daily).
4. Strain
5. Decant into dropper bottles for use.

**<u>Immune boosting Rosemary Tincture</u>**

(Great for your brain, your hair, your skin too)

**Ingredients:** Dried rosemary, vodka.

**Instructions:** Follow the steps above. Take 1 - 2 drops daily

**<u>DIY Calming Rescue Tincture</u>** (For stress, shock, or overwhelm)

**Ingredients:**
- 2 tbsp dried chamomile flowers (calms nerves)
- 1 tbsp fresh lemon balm leaves (soothes anxiety)
- 1 tbsp lavender buds (relaxes mind + body)
- 1 tsp rose petals (comforts heartache)
- 1 cup vodka or brandy (80-proof min.) *or* apple cider vinegar (alcohol-free)
- 1 tbsp vegetable glycerine (optional, for sweetness)
- Small amber glass dropper bottle

**How to Use:**
- **For acute stress:** 2 - 4 drops under tongue, repeat every 10 mins as needed.
- **Daily maintenance:** 2 drops in water/tea, 2xday.
- Store away from sunlight; lasts 2+ years.

**Bonus:**
Add **1 tsp passionflower** (for obsessive worries) or **holy basil** (for adrenal fatigue).

**What herbs and base will you use to create a tincture?**

___________________________________________

___________________________________________

**My Daily Herbal Rituals**

**Herbs are an everyday part of my life. Here's a glimpse of what I use and how I incorporate them into my day:**

**Morning Rituals**
**Cayenne Pepper**
A couple of shakes in water first thing in the morning on an empty stomach. I use it because **I believe** it:
- Prevents blood clots
- Strengthens the heart
- Improves circulation
- Supports elasticity of veins and arteries
- Helps prevent acidity

**Turmeric Shot**
Made with turmeric, ginger, lemon, lemon juice, black pepper, bay leaf, cloves, and water. I take it to:
- Strengthen my immune system
- Fight cancer in my body
- Kill parasites and fungi
- Reduce blood pressure and plaque
- Support joint and bone health
- Improve concentration and focus

**Herbal Tea**
Drunk hot, cold, or blended into smoothies. One pot lasts 1 - 2 days. I create a base blend and then add herbs as needed. The base already includes powerful ingredients:

🌺 **Hibiscus** - Pleasant taste; supports kidney health

🌿 **Nettle** - Adaptogenic; balances stress responses

🧡 **Hawthorn** - Supports heart health

🦴 **Horsetail** - Promotes bone strength

**Hair & Skin Care**

- I use **rosemary and bay leaf-infused** hair products or rinse my hair in rosemary and bay leaf infused water.
- My **homemade lotion** includes **thyme, rosemary, aloe vera, castor oil and frankincense oil** - nourishing and antibacterial.

**On-the-Go Essentials**

I carry a small pill box with compartments.  Instead of pills there are:

- Cloves
- Coriander seeds
- Cayenne pepper
- Rosemary
- Mineral salt

I chew some, sip others, and place a bit of salt under my tongue when needed, for energy, digestion, and mineral support.

*These routines help me stay connected to nature's rhythm and its healing energy. I move through different phases and make changes along the way. It's not about being rigid with your choices, but about enjoying the journey.*

If you're looking for more motivation and trustworthy guidance on natural healing, I highly recommend checking out Dr. Barbara O'Neill and Dr. Eric Berg.

Both have a wealth of educational videos available on YouTube, covering topics like nutrition, detox, hormones, herbal remedies, and the root causes of illness. Their practical, down to earth advice can offer clarity and inspiration as you take steps toward deeper wellness.

## 🌿 My COVID Jab Experience

A few days after my second COVID shot, I woke up with a strange pain.

My baby and ring fingers were so sore I couldn't even touch anything. By the next morning, it was worse. Swollen knuckles, stiffness, heat radiating from the joints. Eventually, every finger joined in, and the pain started waking me up at night.

It felt like my body had hit a tipping point. Instinctively, I reached for what I knew: turmeric and ginger. I started making fresh shots with both, mixing in black pepper and lemon.

What happened next felt nothing short of a miracle. The pain began to ease almost immediately. The swelling went down. And while the baby fingers never fully healed, those knuckles took some real damage, the rest of my hands recovered completely.

Now, every morning, I wake up and wiggle my fingers. They've become my personal inflammation barometer. If they're stiff, swollen, or sore, I know something in my body is off, and it's time to listen and take action.

I still make turmeric-ginger shots every morning. It's simple, powerful, and a ritual of self-care that reminds me: healing doesn't always come in the form of a prescription. It's all around us, woven into nature.

✎ **Have you ever noticed your body "speaking" to you through pain or discomfort? What did it try to say?**

_______________________________________________

_______________________________________________

**What are your inflammation signals?** *(e.g., puffy hands, joint pain, skin flare ups, brain fog)*

_______________________________________________

_______________________________________________

**Are there foods or natural remedies you turn to when you feel out of balance?**

_______________________________________________

_______________________________________________

**What morning rituals or check-ins could help you stay in tune with your body?**

_______________________________________________

_______________________________________________

*What does "healing through food" mean to me?*

_______________________________________________

_______________________________________________

**Final Note:**

This chapter invites you to reflect on how food makes you feel, what your body may be asking for, and how to begin shifting toward nourishment, gently, intuitively, and at your own pace.

Herbs and spices are more than flavour, they are medicine woven into daily life. Whether you're sipping a calming tea, stirring spices into a warm meal, or crafting your own tincture, these simple rituals connect you to the rhythms of nature and the quiet wisdom of your body.

Healing doesn't have to be complicated. One leaf, one flower, one drop at a time, you begin to restore balance.

Let every small act of care, every meal, every cup of tea, be a reminder: you are already on the path.

# Chapter Six: The Power of Fermented Foods

*Fermentation isn't just about preserving food, it's about restoring life to our meals and healing our inner ecosystem.*

**The Magic of Fermentation**

For someone who's not only a self-proclaimed lousy cook but also finds cooking thoroughly unrewarding, it might come as a surprise that there's almost always something bubbling away in our kitchen.

I absolutely love fermenting! There's something deeply satisfying, even magical, about transforming simple fruit and vegetables into delicious, healing creations. Despite my aversion to cooking, fermenting feels like an act of creativity and self-care.

It's alive, intentional, and rooted in tradition.

Fermented foods have been used for centuries as natural remedies to support digestion, strengthen the immune system, and promote overall wellbeing. Long before modern medicine and refrigeration, our ancestors understood the powerful health benefits of fermentation, not only as a method of preservation but also as a source of nourishment and healing.

**The Ancient Art of Fermentation**

Before fridges and freezers, people relied on fermentation to keep their food safe, not just for days, but through whole seasons. Whether it was vegetables, grains, dairy, or even meat, they learned to use good bacteria and yeasts to transform fresh food into something tangy, nourishing, and long-lasting.

In times of war or hardship, fermented foods were more than just a meal, they were lifesavers. Families would hide jars of pickled vegetables, cultured dairy, olives, and preserved meats in stone cellars or even bury them underground to keep them from being stolen. These foods became part of their survival toolkit.

And it wasn't just about staying full. Fermented foods are packed with probiotics, enzymes, and vitamins, the kind of natural nutrition that helped people avoid scurvy, malnutrition, and other illnesses when fresh produce and medicine were hard to find.

Soldiers and families alike turned to these powerful, living foods to stay strong, fend off sickness, and boost resilience.

It's incredible to think of fermented foods not just as tasty sides, but as homemade, living medicine. A reminder that sometimes the simplest things are also the most powerful.

**What Fermented Foods Can Heal**

Thanks to their probiotic and enzyme-rich composition, fermented foods have been shown to help manage and even reverse a variety of chronic and inflammatory health conditions. Some of the common conditions that may benefit from regular consumption of fermented foods include:

- Irritable bowel syndrome (IBS) and digestive disorders
- Candida overgrowth and yeast infections
- Eczema and other skin conditions
- Chronic fatigue and brain fog
- Allergies and food sensitivities
- Autoimmune disorders
- Menopausal symptoms such as hot flashes, mood swings, and hormonal imbalance
- Obesity and weight management issues
- Type 2 diabetes and insulin resistance

By restoring gut flora and reducing systemic inflammation, fermented foods can serve as a foundational element of functional nutrition and holistic healing.

**Exploring Your Relationship with Fermented Foods**

**What fermented foods, if any, are currently part of my diet?** (e.g., yogurt, kimchi, kefir, sauerkraut, kombucha, miso, pickles)

______________________________________________

______________________________________________

**What motivated me to start eating fermented foods, or what's held me back?** (Have I heard they're healthy? Or do they seem strange or intimidating?)

______________________________________________

______________________________________________

**Do I notice any changes in digestion, energy, skin, or mood when I include fermented foods regularly?** (How does my body respond?)

______________________________________________

______________________________________________

**Have I ever made my own fermented foods?** What was that experience like? If not, does the idea excite or intimidate me?

______________________________________________

______________________________________________

**How do I think my gut health is affecting my overall wellbeing right now?** (Energy levels, immune system, mood, skin, or digestion?)

______________________________________________

______________________________________________

**How Fermented Foods Work**

Fermentation is basically nature's way of preserving food and upgrading it. During this process, beneficial bacteria and yeasts break things down and boost the nutritional benefits at the same time. It's a win-win. Your food stays fresh longer *and* becomes way more nourishing.

The result is tangy, probiotic-rich foods that do more than just taste good, they work quietly behind the scenes to restore balance and support your whole system.

Instead of simply eating to feel full, you're now eating to nourish, and that's a big shift. These tangy, probiotic-rich foods work quietly behind the scenes to support your whole system.

**Why Probiotics Matter**

Your gut is home to trillions of microbes that affect nearly every part of your wellbeing, from how you digest and absorb nutrients to how you fight off illness and even how you feel emotionally.

Fermented foods are one of the simplest and most natural ways to replenish those friendly microbes. When they're in balance, you feel more balanced too.

**Here's what probiotics can help with:**

- **Digestion:** Less bloating, better breakdown of food
- **Immunity:** Strengthens your natural defences
- **Nutrient absorption:** Helps your body get more from your meals
- **Inflammation:** Calms internal stress and supports healing
- **Mood & brain health:** Supports clarity and calm through the gut-brain connection
- **Weight and blood sugar:** Helps reduce cravings and regulate metabolism

But modern life, full of stress, antibiotics, processed food, and environmental toxins, often throws this delicate microbial balance off. That's when trouble begins:

- Tummy problems
- Weakened immune defences
- Increased inflammation
- Low mood and brain fog
- Sluggish metabolism

Adding fermented foods is a simple, natural way to **feed your good bugs,** rebuild your resilience, and restore harmony to your inner ecosystem.

## What About Hidden Infections?

Not all bugs announce themselves. Some hang around quietly, parasites, viruses, yeast, even mould, and over time, they can chip away at your energy, mood, and immune function. They can hide, lay eggs, and reemerge if your body isn't strong enough to keep them in check.

Some integrative practitioners believe that many chronic illnesses (even some types of cancer) may have microbial roots. And while this is still being explored in mainstream science, the idea that hidden infections contribute to long term imbalance is gaining ground.

**How Fermented Foods Help Fight the Bad Guys**

Fermented foods don't just add good bacteria, they help **defend** you from the bad ones. They:

- **Crowd out harmful microbes** by taking up space and resources
- **Lower gut pH**, making the environment less hospitable to invaders
- **Produce enzymes and natural antibacterials** that break down toxins
- **Support your immune system**, keeping your body alert and responsive

When your gut is populated with helpful, living microbes, you feel clearer, lighter, stronger, and more connected to your body.

So next time you're sipping on kefir, tossing sauerkraut onto a salad, or enjoying a spoonful of miso, remember: you're not just eating, **you're healing**.

Some studies even link certain long term infections to bigger health problems like cancer. These aren't the kind of bugs that just go away with one round of treatment. Some lay eggs or go into hiding, so they can come back if your system's out of balance.

**Some common troublemakers include:**

- **Candida**. Sugar-loving yeast that thrives after antibiotics
- **H. pylori**. Often linked to ulcers and reflux
- **E. coli & Salmonella**. Can stick around after food poisoning
- **Parasites**. Like worms or tiny one-cell bugs
- **Viruses**. Like Epstein-Barr, which may cause fatigue

**More Interesting Things to Know...**

Here is another titbit *worth noting*, especially if you're someone who likes to dig into the "why" behind things:

🌀 **Parasites and Cancer. Is There a Link?**

There's growing talk in some health circles about how certain parasites might be connected to cancer. It's not totally mainstream yet, but some researchers and practitioners have noticed that people dealing with chronic illness, including cancer, often also have underlying parasite issues.

This might explain the recent buzz around meds like **fenbendazole** (yes, originally for deworming animals) and **ivermectin** being explored for human use beyond their usual roles. While it's still a bit controversial, it's sparked interest in how microbes and parasites might play a bigger part in long term illness than we once thought.

**Herbs and Spice: Nature's Antimicrobials**

In tandem with fermented foods, certain herbs and spice have long been used in traditional medicine to disarm pathogens and kill their eggs, as well as strengthen the body's defences. Many contain powerful compounds with natural antimicrobial, antifungal, antiparasitic, or antiviral properties. These include:

💀 **Powerful Cleanser**
Black Walnut & Wormwood - Traditional parasite eliminators

🍍 **Enzyme Attackers**
Pineapple - Contains bromelain to break down invaders

🥄 **Growth Disruptors**
Papaya Seeds - Paralyses parasites' digestive systems

🔥 **Lifecycle Killers**
Clove - Destroys eggs and larvae
Pumpkin Seeds - Contains cucurbitacin to paralyze worms

🛡 **Broad-Spectrum Warriors**
Garlic - Antibacterial, antiviral, and antiparasitic
Thyme - Fights fungi and parasites

🌱 **Gut Healers**
Ginger & Turmeric - Soothe inflammation and bacterial imbalance
Liquorice Root & Olive Leaf - Support immune defence and detox

Incorporating these herbs into your meals, teas, or tinctures can help your body gently cleanse and guard against microbial threats.

<u>**Anti-Pathogen Purifying Tea**</u>

**Purpose:** Designed to help the body combat parasites, fungal overgrowth, and harmful microbes while supporting the immune system and reducing inflammation.

**Ingredients (Makes 2 servings)**
- 1 tsp dried wormwood *(bitter, use sparingly and not long term)*
- ½ tsp black walnut hull *(dried or tincture form; skip if allergic to nuts)*
- 1 tsp dried thyme
- ½ tsp ground clove *(or 2 whole cloves)*
- 1 tsp grated fresh ginger
- 1 tsp grated fresh turmeric *(or ½ tsp powder)*
- 1 clove garlic, crushed
- 1 tsp pumpkin seeds, crushed
- ½ tsp papaya seeds, dried and ground
- ½ cup fresh pineapple chunks *(or ¼ cup juice added after steeping)*
- ½ tsp liquorice root *(avoid if you have high blood pressure)*
- ½ tsp olive leaf

**Instructions** - Prepare a decoction base:
1. In a pot, combine wormwood, black walnut, thyme, clove, liquorice root, olive leaf, ginger, turmeric, and garlic with 3 cups of water. Bring to a boil, then reduce heat and let simmer gently for 15 - 20 minutes.
2. Add pineapple and papaya seeds: Remove from heat. Add pineapple chunks (or wait to add juice after it cools slightly) and papaya seeds. Let steep for 10 more minutes, covered.
3. Strain: Strain the tea into a cup. Add crushed pumpkin seeds just before drinking for maximum enzyme and nutrient content.
4. Optional Additions: Add raw honey or squeeze a bit of lemon to brighten the flavour.

**Use With Care:**

- Do **not use wormwood or black walnut long term** (max 2 weeks) without guidance from a qualified practitioner.
- Avoid if pregnant, breastfeeding, or on immunosuppressant medications.
- Start with small amounts and observe your body's response. Make notes.

✋ *Always consult with a qualified herbalist or healthcare provider before using medicinal herbs, especially in concentrated form. Some herbs may interact with medications or underlying health conditions.*

**Natto: Japan's Fermented Superfood**

No chapter on fermented foods would be complete without mentioning **natto**, a traditional Japanese dish made from fermented soybeans.

Legend has it that natto was discovered accidentally when boiled soybeans, stored in straw by soldiers, were left for several days and began to ferment naturally. What emerged was a sticky, stringy, and pungent food with incredible health benefits.

Natto contains **nattokinase**, an enzyme that has been shown to break down blood clots and clear cholesterol from arteries, making it a powerful ally for heart health ad highly recommended by Dr Eric Berg. That said, a word of warning, its appearance is not for the faint hearted. Personally, I couldn't get past the slimy texture, even though the taste is actually quite mild. Still, it's a beloved staple in Japan, and for good reason.

**Foods That Are Easy to Ferment**

If you're just beginning your fermentation journey, there are a number of foods that are particularly easy to start with:

- **Cabbage** - for making sauerkraut or kimchi. It ferments quickly and requires only salt and time.
- **Cucumbers** - simple to turn into pickles with brine, garlic, and spices.
- **Carrots** - crunchy, sweet, and ideal for fermenting with ginger or dill.
- **Beets** - earthy and vibrant, beets ferment beautifully on their own or mixed with other vegetables.
- **Yogurt** - made from milk and a starter culture, a great introduction to dairy fermentation.
- **Kefir** - another probiotic rich dairy option, easy to make at home with kefir grains.
- **Kombucha** - fermented tea that's slightly fizzy and full of gut friendly bacteria.
- **Ginger beer** - a naturally fermented, slightly sweet beverage that's easy to prepare.
- **Garlic cloves** - fermented garlic mellows in flavour and becomes both delicious and medicinal. Don't be alarmed if they turn blue. This can happen as part of a chemical reaction to the changing PH levels.
- **Turmeric root** - often added to vegetable ferments or brines for its Anti-inflammatory benefits and vibrant colour.
- **Ginger root** - enhances flavour and provides additional digestive support when added to ferments.

These beginner friendly ferments typically require minimal ingredients and equipment. Most only need salt, clean jars, and a bit of patience.

**Foods That Should Not Be Fermented**

While many foods lend themselves well to fermentation, some are best avoided either due to safety concerns or poor results:

- **Meat and seafood**. These can be fermented safely only under strict traditional or industrial methods (e.g., fish sauce, fermented sausage). Home fermentation poses a risk of harmful bacterial contamination.
- **Foods with preservatives**, such as vinegar packed pickles or canned goods. Preservatives inhibit microbial activity needed for fermentation.
- **Heavily processed or sugary foods** which can promote the growth of undesirable bacteria or yeast rather than beneficial strains.
- **Overripe or mouldy produce** while fermentation discourages harmful microbes, starting with spoiled food increases contamination risks.

Where possible stick with fresh, organic, and chemical free ingredients to ensure safe, high quality ferments.

**A Personal Turning Point**

Though I had always enjoyed fermented foods, they weren't something I intentionally consumed every day until life demanded it. I began to notice changes in my body. Something felt off. I started experiencing hot flushes and other symptoms that didn't quite make sense.

Around the same time, I was attending a year-long hypnotherapy and counselling course every weekend, and one of the participants noticed my symptoms and recommended a holistic doctor. That recommendation was life changing.

The doctor ran an **Oligoscan** test, which revealed my body was completely out of balance. It was prior to the cancer diagnosis, and although I didn't know what was coming, I had a strong subconscious sense that something needed my attention. I had become meticulous, almost obsessive, about what I ate, trying to tune into my body's signals.

During our sessions, the doctor guided me to make additional key lifestyle changes particularly in relation to what went in and on my body. She opened my eyes to the profound role of fermented foods in restoring balance and vitality.

She explained that true health is all about balance, and that balance begins in the spine and the digestive tract. When these foundational systems are "off," the entire body suffers, primarily through the mechanism of inflammation.

Many holistic practitioners now believe that there's no such thing as disease in the traditional sense, only different manifestations of chronic inflammation. From this perspective, conditions like cancer are seen not as random afflictions but as the end result of long term imbalance.

Fermented foods, with their probiotic rich  content, are essential tools in the fight against inflammation alongside other powerful natural allies like turmeric, ginger, and medicinal herbs.

**Fermented Foods Today: Functional Medicine in Disguise**
In contrast to the vibrant, living foods of the past, much of the food available today is overprocessed, chemically treated, and essentially "dead." These foods are stripped of their enzymes, beneficial microbes, and life giving energy. As a result, our digestion weakens, immune defences falter, and overall vitality declines.

That's why fermented foods feel so essential to me now. They are living foods, tangy, sometimes sour, and always full of life. Their bold flavours signal that something deeply alive is happening. From sauerkraut to yogurt, kombucha to ginger beer, these traditional foods are functional medicine in disguise.

## ✍️ My Current Relationship With Fermented Foods

Let's take a moment to check in, are fermented foods already part of your day, or are they still sitting on your "someday" list?

**What fermented foods am I curious to try?** (Yogurt? Kimchi? Kefir? Sauerkraut? Tempeh?)

_______________________________________________

_______________________________________________

**How could these foods support my body or gut health?** (More energy? Happier digestion? Better immunity?)

_______________________________________________

_______________________________________________

**Where could I naturally add fermented foods into meals I already enjoy?** (Salad topper? Smoothie base? A tangy side?)

_______________________________________________

_______________________________________________

**What's one small, simple step I can take this week to add more living, healing foods to my plate?** (Buy a jar? Try a spoonful a day? Learn one easy recipe?)

_______________________________________________

_______________________________________________

**Easy Fermented Recipes to Try at Home**

You don't need fancy equipment or skills to start fermenting at home. Here are some simple recipes to get you started:

**<u>Homemade Yogurt Recipe</u> (Using Shop Bought or Previous Batch as Starter)**

**Ingredients:**
- 1 litre whole milk
- 2 tablespoons plain yogurt (with live active cultures)

**Equipment:**
- Heavy-bottomed saucepan
- Spoon or whisk
- Thermometer (optional but helpful)
- Clean glass or ceramic container with lid or cover

**Instructions:**
- **Heat the Milk:** Pour the milk into a saucepan and slowly heat it till it almost boils.
- **Cool the Milk:** Allow the milk to cool. The milk should feel warm to the touch but not hot.
- **Add the Starter Yogurt:** Take 2 tablespoons of plain yogurt and mix it with a bit of the cooled milk in a small bowl to thin it out. Then stir this mixture back into the rest of the milk. Mix gently but thoroughly.
- **Ferment:** Pour into a clean container. Cover it with a lid or clean cloth and place it in a warm, undisturbed spot (like an oven with the light on, a yogurt maker, or a warm shelf). Let it sit for **6 to 12 hours**, depending on how tangy and thick you like it.
- **Chill:** Once set, move the yogurt to the refrigerator for at least 2 hours before eating. This helps thicken the texture further.

**Tips:**
- Save 2 tablespoons of your homemade yogurt as a starter for your next batch.
- You can flavour the yogurt after it's set with honey, fruit, or herbs.

## <u>Beet Kvass</u> (Earthy, Salty Ferment)

Beet kvass is a nutrient dense tonic that supports liver health and detoxification.

**Ingredients:**
- 2 - 3 beets, chopped
- 1 tbsp sea salt
- 1 Litre water
- Optional: garlic, ginger, bay leaf, or spices

**Instructions:**
- Place chopped beets in a jar.
- Dissolve salt in water and pour over the beets.
- Add optional spices if desired.
- Cover loosely and ferment at room temperature for 3 - 7 days.
- Strain and store in the fridge.

**To Use:**
Drink 1 - 2 tablespoons daily for liver and blood support.

<u>**Quick Carrot/Radish Brine Pickles**</u>

These crunchy pickles are a great way to add fermented veggies to your meals.

**Ingredients:**
- Sliced carrots or radishes
- 2% sea salt
- 2 cups filtered water

**Instructions:**
1. Pack sliced veggies tightly into a clean jar.
2. Dissolve salt in water to make a brine.
3. Pour brine over the veggies, ensuring they're fully submerged.
4. Weight them down with a fermentation weight or small jar.
5. Ferment at room temperature for 3 - 5 days, then refrigerate.

Bonus Tip: Use the leftover brine in salad dressings, soups, or as a digestive tonic.  It's full of probiotics!

## Ginger Bug & Ginger Beer

A ginger bug is a natural starter culture for making fizzy, probiotic rich, delicious ginger beer

**Ingredients and Instructions:**

- 1 tbsp grated ginger
- 1 tbsp sugar
- ½ cup filtered water

1. Stir all ingredients together in a jar.
2. Feed it 1 tbsp ginger and 1 tbsp sugar daily for 5 - 7 days until bubbly and fragrant.

## Ginger Beer Recipe:

- ½ cup ginger bug
- ½ cup fresh ginger
- ½ - ¾ cup sugar
- Juice of 1 lemon
- 7 cups water

1. Simmer ginger, sugar, and water until dissolved. Cool completely.
2. Strain and mix with ginger bug and lemon juice.
3. Bottle and ferment at room temperature for 2 - 4 days, burping daily to release pressure.
4. Chill before serving.

Note:
Don't let it ferment too long as it can turn into alcohol or vinegar! Unless that's the point!

## Sourdough Starter & Bread

Sourdough is another fermented food that's gentle on the gut and delicious.

Sourdough Starter Instructions:

- ½ cup flour + ½ cup water

1. Mix flour and water in a jar.
2. Feed daily by discarding half and adding fresh flour and water.
3. Repeat for 5 - 7 days until bubbly and active.

Simple Sourdough Bread Recipe:

- 1 cup active starter
- 3 cups flour
- 1¼ cups water
- 1½ tsp salt

1. Mix all ingredients and knead until smooth.
2. Let rise for 4 - 6 hours or overnight.
3. Shape into a loaf and bake at 220°C / 425°F for 30 - 35 minutes.

### Bonus Tips for Fermenting Success

1. Keep It Clean: Always use clean jars, utensils, and hands to prevent contamination.
2. Submerge Veggies: Ensure vegetables are fully submerged in brine to avoid mould.
3. Trust Your Senses: If it smells off or looks mouldy, discard it. Healthy ferments should smell tangy and pleasant.
4. Start Small: Begin with small amounts of fermented foods to allow your body to adjust.

<u>**Classic Sauerkraut Recipe**</u> *(Simple, Tangy, Probiotic rich )*

**Ingredients:**
- 1 medium green cabbage
- Mineral salt (rule of thumb with fermenting is **2% of the cabbage weight**)

**Instructions:**
1. **Prepare the cabbage:** Remove outer leaves, then thinly slice or shred the cabbage. (Save a couple of the big outer leaves to put on top to submerge the shredded cabbage.)
2. **Massage with salt:** Place shredded cabbage in a large bowl, sprinkle salt evenly over it. Massage and squeeze the cabbage with your hands for about 5 - 10 minutes until it starts releasing liquid and softens.
3. **Add flavour (optional):** Mix in caraway seeds or juniper berries if using.
4. **Pack tightly:** Transfer the cabbage and its liquid into a clean glass jar or fermentation crock. Press down firmly to eliminate air pockets; the liquid should cover the cabbage. If not enough juice, add a little salted water (1 tsp salt per cup water).
5. **Weigh it down:** Place the saved big outer cabbage leaves on top and then put a fermentation weight or a smaller jar filled with water on top to keep cabbage submerged. Cover loosely with a cloth or a fermentation lid to allow gases to escape but prevent contamination.
6. **Ferment:** Keep at room temperature for 1 - 8 weeks. Check daily to ensure cabbage stays submerged, skim any scum if needed. Taste after 1 week and ferment longer for stronger flavour.
7. **Store:** When you like the taste, seal with a lid and refrigerate. It will keep for several months.

**Have Some Fun: Flavour Additions for Your Sauerkraut**

**Spices & Seeds**
- **Black peppercorns** - subtle heat and earthy depth
- **Bay leaves** - aromatic and slightly floral; also antimicrobial
- **Caraway seeds** - classic, warm, and anise-like flavour
- **Mustard seeds** - tangy and mildly spicy
- **Fennel seeds** - sweet and liquorice-like; aids digestion
- **Coriander seeds** - citrusy and fragrant
- **Celery seeds** - savoury, slightly bitter, and aromatic

**Roots**
- **Garlic cloves** - antimicrobial, Immune boosting, and flavourful
- **Ginger root (sliced or grated)** - warming, anti-inflammatory, and zesty
- **Turmeric root (sliced or grated)** - earthy, vibrant colour, and anti-inflammatory
- **Horseradish** - spicy, pungent, and great for clearing sinuses

**Vegetables & Fruit**
- **Carrots (julienned)** - sweet crunch and colour
- **Beets (shredded)** - earthy sweetness and vivid pink hue
- **Radish (sliced or shredded)** - peppery and crunchy
- **Apple (sliced or grated)** - a hint of sweetness
- **Onion (thinly sliced)** - deeper savoury flavour
- **Chili peppers** - for heat and metabolic boost

**Herbs (Fresh or Dried)**
- **Dill** - classic in pickling, adds fresh, grassy notes
- **Parsley** - mild and cleansing
- **Thyme** - earthy and antimicrobial
- **Rosemary** - piney and aromatic
- **Oregano** - bold, slightly bitter, and antimicrobial

<u>**Spicy Kimchi Recipe**</u>

*(Korean-Style Fermented Veggies with Heat)*

**Ingredients:**
- 1 medium Chinese cabbage (about 2 lbs)
- ¼ cup sea salt
- 4 cups water
- 1 tbsp grated ginger
- 3 garlic cloves, minced
- 2 tbsp fish sauce (or soy sauce for vegan)
- 1 tbsp sugar or sweetener
- 3 - 4 tbsp Korean red chili flakes (adjust for heat preference)
- 3 scallions, chopped
- 1 medium carrot, julienned
- 1 small daikon radish, julienned (optional)

**Instructions:**
1. **Salt the cabbage:** Chop cabbage into bite-sized pieces. Dissolve salt in water and soak cabbage in this brine for 2 - 4 hours, tossing occasionally. Drain and rinse cabbage well to remove excess salt.
2. **Make the spice paste:** Mix garlic, ginger, fish sauce (or soy sauce), sugar, and chili flakes in a bowl. Add a little water if needed to make a thick paste.
3. **Combine veggies:** In a large bowl, mix drained cabbage, scallions, carrot, and daikon. Add the spice paste and use gloves to thoroughly coat all the vegetables.
4. **Pack into jar:** Transfer to a clean jar, pressing down to remove air pockets and ensure vegetables are submerged. Leave about 1 - 2 inches of space at the top.
5. **Ferment:** Cover loosely with cloth or fermentation lid. Leave at room temperature for 3 - 7 days, tasting daily. Once it reaches desired sourness, seal with a lid and refrigerate. Kimchi will continue to develop flavour over time.

<u>**Fermented Cucumbers**</u>

**Ingredients:**
- 4 - 5 small cucumbers
- 3 cups filtered water
- 2 tbsp sea salt or Himalayan salt
- 3 - 4 garlic cloves, smashed
- 1 tsp black peppercorns
- A few fresh dill sprigs (or 1 tbsp dried dill)
- Optional: 1 bay leaf, pinch of red chili flakes for heat

**Instructions:**
1. **Prepare the brine:** Dissolve salt in water, stirring until fully dissolved. This creates a salty brine to encourage good bacteria growth and prevent bad bacteria.
2. **Prepare cucumbers:** Wash cucumbers well. Trim off the blossom ends (they contain enzymes that can cause softening).
3. **Pack the jar:** Place garlic, peppercorns, dill, and any optional spices at the bottom of a clean glass jar (1 quart size works well). Pack the cucumbers tightly in the jar, leaving about 1 inch of headspace at the top.
4. **Add brine:** Pour the salty brine over the cucumbers, making sure they're fully submerged. Use a fermentation weight or a clean small jar to keep cucumbers under the brine and avoid exposure to air.
5. **Cover and ferment:** Cover the jar loosely with a lid or cloth to allow gases to escape. Leave the jar at room temperature (around 65 - 75°F or 18 - 24°C) out of direct sunlight.
6. **Fermentation time:** Let the cucumbers ferment for 5 - 10 days. Check daily to ensure cucumbers stay submerged and skim off any white scum if it appears (this is harmless).
7. **Taste test:** Start tasting after day 5. When the cucumbers have reached the tangy, sour flavour you like, transfer the jar to the fridge to slow fermentation. They'll keep for several months refrigerated.

Experiment by adding mustard seeds, coriander seeds, or fresh herbs like tarragon.

**Incorporating Fermented Foods Into Daily Life**

Fermented foods don't have to be intimidating. They can easily fit into your routine. Here are some ideas:

- Add sauerkraut or kimchi to salads, grain bowls, or sandwiches.
- Blend kefir into smoothies for a probiotic boost.
- Drink beet kvass as a morning tonic or midday pick-me-up.
- Use sourdough bread instead of regular bread for easier digestion.

**Final Reflection: Healing Through Fermentation**

Fermentation is more than a process, it's a reminder of nature's resilience and wisdom. By embracing these ancient practices, we reconnect with our roots and give our bodies the tools they need to thrive.

*How has my relationship with food changed now that I see it as alive and healing?*

___________________________________________

___________________________________________

*What recipes am I keen to try now?*

___________________________________________

___________________________________________

**Wrapping Up Section One: Food as Fuel, Medicine, and Magic**

Everything you've read in this first section is about one simple truth: food is powerful. When we get intentional about what we put into our bodies, from vibrant juices and nourishing smoothies to healing soups, broths, herbs, spices, and fermented foods, we're not just eating. We're replenishing, restoring, and realigning.

Every ingredient has a purpose. Every choice becomes a message to your body. And when you eat with awareness, you begin to feel the difference, not just physically, but emotionally and energetically too.

As we move forward, the journey continues beyond the plate. In the next section, we'll explore what we put **onto** our bodies; natural skincare, mindful self-care, and ways to nurture your body from the outside in.

And after that, we'll dive into the mind-body connection, energy healing, and tools to cultivate lasting wellness in every aspect of your life.

So, let's keep going. There's so much more goodness to come.

# Your Food Journal: Reflect, Realign, Reconnect

I recently broke the rules and ate fast food in between meetings. I was rushed, hungry, and made a snap decision. Within minutes (and I mean *minutes*), I was sweating, sluggish, and barely able to keep my eyes open. Thankfully, I was close to home. I cancelled my meeting, drove back, sank into a chair, and didn't wake up for three hours.

Now, obviously, that's an extreme reaction, but it's also a powerful reminder. Our bodies are constantly communicating with us, sending signals in response to what we feed them. The question is: **are we listening?**

That's what this journal is for. Not just to track what you eat, but to explore how it makes you feel, physically, emotionally, and energetically. Did that green smoothie lift your mood? Did that heavy dinner drain your energy? Did you feel clear and calm, or foggy and bloated?

Start to notice the patterns. Start to hear the quiet messages your body is sending. Start to make food choices that nourish you, not just fuel you.

This space is yours. Use it to record what you eat, how you feel afterward, and any shifts you notice over time.

Note the meals that leave you feeling vibrant and the ones that leave you depleted. Write down the foods you want to add more of, and the ones you might be ready to let go.

Healing begins with awareness. And awareness begins here, one bite, one choice, one journal page at a time.

**Weekly Food Journal - Week 1**

**Date Range:** _______________________________

| Day | What I Ate | How I Felt/Notes |
| --- | --- | --- |
| Mon | | |
| Tues | | |
| Wed | | |
| Thurs | | |
| Fri | | |
| Sat | | |
| Sun | | |
| Notes: | | |
| | | |

*What foods made me feel most nourished this week?*

_______________________________________________

_______________________________________________

*Did I notice any patterns in my energy, mood, or digestion?*

_______________________________________________

_______________________________________________

*Was I eating mindfully, or out of habit/emotion/stress?*

_______________________________________________

_______________________________________________

*What is one thing I want to try or adjust next week?*

_______________________________________________

_______________________________________________

***Next Week's Intention:*** *(Write one or two small steps or focuses for the week ahead)*

_______________________________________________

_______________________________________________

_______________________________________________

_______________________________________________

**Weekly Food Journal - Week 2**

**Date Range:** _______________________________

| Day | What I Ate | How I Felt/Notes |
|---|---|---|
| **Mon** | | |
| **Tues** | | |
| **Wed** | | |
| **Thurs** | | |
| **Fri** | | |
| **Sat** | | |
| **Sun** | | |
| **Notes:** | | |
| | | |

*How did my body feel when I woke up each day?*

_________________________________________________

_________________________________________________

*Did I eat in a calm environment or while distracted (phone, TV, rushing)?*

_________________________________________________

_________________________________________________

*What cravings did I notice, and what might they be telling me?*

_________________________________________________

_________________________________________________

*How did my food choices affect my sleep or focus?*

_________________________________________________

_________________________________________________

*Next Week's Intention:* (Write one or two small steps or focuses for the week ahead)

_________________________________________________

_________________________________________________

_________________________________________________

_________________________________________________

**Weekly Food Journal - Week 3**

**Date Range:** _________________________

| Day | What I Ate | How I Felt/Notes |
|---|---|---|
| **Mon** | | |
| **Tues** | | |
| **Wed** | | |
| **Thurs** | | |
| **Fri** | | |
| **Sat** | | |
| **Sun** | | |
| **Notes:** | | |
| | | |

*What am I most proud of this week?*

______________________________________________

______________________________________________

*What foods made me feel good this week?*

______________________________________________

______________________________________________

*Were there any meals I regretted or reacted to?*

______________________________________________

______________________________________________

*What's one small thing I want to try next week?*

______________________________________________

______________________________________________

***Next Week's Intention:*** *(Write one or two small steps or focuses for the week ahead)*

______________________________________________

______________________________________________

______________________________________________

______________________________________________

## Weekly Food Journal - Week 4

**Date Range:** _______________________________

| Day | What I Ate | How I Felt/Notes |
|---|---|---|
| **Mon** | | |
| **Tues** | | |
| **Wed** | | |
| **Thurs** | | |
| **Fri** | | |
| **Sat** | | |
| **Sun** | | |
| **Notes:** | | |
| | | |

**Final Reflection After 4 Weeks**

*How has my relationship with food changed this month?*

_______________________________________________

_______________________________________________

*What new habits or discoveries surprised me?*

_______________________________________________

_______________________________________________

*Which foods truly nourish me - body, mind, and soul?*

_______________________________________________

_______________________________________________

*What do I want to carry forward into the next part of my wellness journey?*

_______________________________________________

_______________________________________________

www.ingramcontent.com/pod-product-compliance
Lightning Source LLC
Chambersburg PA
CBHW071154300726
48975CB00004B/1147